Alki

A NOVEL

Christopher Anderson

ISBN: **1492212725**
ISBN 13: **9781492212720**

I dedicate this novel to my wife, Nancy.

"There are open wounds, shrunk sometimes to the size of a pin-prick
but wounds still."
F. Scott Fitzgerald, *Tender is the Night*

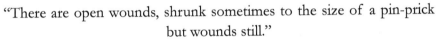

The following is a work of fiction. Any similarity to persons alive or
dead is coincidental.

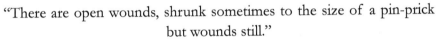

ONE

It was a super sunny Sunday in July, 1968. Jackson McMahon and Peter Placik were cruising Alki Beach in Peter's 1962 VW Bus, dual exhaust, bored and stroked, observing young sunbathing beauties as any young heterosexual might, testosterone ready, hormones peaking. They sparked the silver sand like temptress sirens; and the ones up on the sidewalk too, in perennial white shorts that (thank you, Lord) got shorter each summer, tight against taut tushes, barely touching tanned thighs. Jackson's and Peter's heads turned on a spindle at a queue of teenage bicyclists, their tight little rear ends reeling up and down on their seats like machine précised gears.

"It should be a crime," twenty-one-year old Jackson said.

"I think it already is," replied twenty-year-old Peter. "What are they—fourteen?"

Two blondes on the sand sprang to their feet and waved frantically. Jackson and Peter waved back.

"Who are they?" Peter said.

"Nobody," Jackson said with a sigh. "My sister is all, and her roommate."

Peter made a sudden screeching u-turn on Alki Avenue.

"What the hell?" Jackson said.

"We're going back."

"She's my sister, goddammit!"

"In an itsy bitsy teeny weensy white bikini!"

"Hands off, you worthless cad!"

The two young ladies in question sat up straight as they saw Peter and Jackson pull up at the curb, jump out and hop across the hot sand barefoot. It was obvious which one was the sister, the one with the long strawberry-blonde hair and brown summer freckles, just like Jackson. Nevertheless, Jackson marched straight up to the other and kissed her sweetly on the lips then collapsed beside her on the blue beach towel, erupting with his customary meaningless chatter as if he were expected to fill a verbal void. The girls responded with short, polite cackles.

Peter said nothing, too full of himself to bother with rhetoric, comfortable in his lean muscular six-foot-two-inch frame, staring numbly across the bay, his head empty of thought, stoned to the gills, numb; shy actually.

"Who's your friend?" someone said vaguely, a voice far away.

"Peter," Jackson said. "Peter Peter peeder eater."

More polite cackles, at Peter's expense, he thought self-consciously.

He meandered over and fell down across from the three, crossing his legs Buddha style.

"I'm Josephine," one said, "and that's Caitlin."

He addressed Jackson's sister with a seductive smile. "Hi."

Caitlin looked back with an open-mouthed question mark planted on her freckled face. Josephine laughed and Jackson shook his head.

"Your friend's a real wit, isn't he?" Josephine said.

"Yeah," Jackson said, "a real ladies' man."

And now Peter blushed, no longer so confident, tongue-tied, and back in Vietnam.

"What do you do, Peter?" Josephine said, trying to hold in the toke off a joint just rolled while passing it on to Jackson.

"He does the same thing I do," Jackson said, and simulated masturbation.

Laughter.

"I'm on *vacaciones*," Peter said.

Jackson shook his head again and sighed. "Two years of high school Spanish and he thinks he knows everything."

Peter blushed again and looked back across the bay to downtown Seattle. The familiar pungent pot odor deodorized the stagnant, smoggy summer bay.

"*Muy bueno, muchacho*," Josephine said, laughing.

Caitlin started giggling.

They piled into Peter's van, Josephine in the back with Jackson, Caitlin up in front in the passenger seat.

"You in the service?" she now blurted out, as far as he knew, her first words ever.

The haircut gave him away every time.

"Just got out."

He'd been drafted and gone over not expecting all that much. His dad had been in Europe during World War II, and the Americans and Germans had shot over each other's heads, Dad had said. Nobody wanted to hurt anyone, Dad had explained. Face to face with the enemy, they made about faces and walked away. It might have been different in the South Pacific with the Japs, he didn't know, since they were the ones that started it all. But the Germans looked just like them. His dad sympathized with the Germans and hated Japs.

So he hadn't expected a whole bunch of really pissed off gooks. And actually it had been calm for awhile—months in fact, boring as hell. Then the hot shit hit the proverbial fan, and it suddenly was all ear-splitting noise and chaos, elbows and assholes, yellow clouds of Orange, leeches, and malaria, the later of which got him an early out. But before that was to happen, it was bubbling blood out of headless necks and arms and genitals blown away. War was real, and he hadn't really thought about it that much beforehand, standing there saying goodbye to Mom and Dad, feeling silly holding a toothbrush, Mom with tears in her eyes for some reason, Dad smiling good-naturedly. It had happened so fast he hadn't had time to consider his predicament, and that "war is wrong," not until the discharge date raised its anticipatory head: "Short!" he'd yell at fellow comrades smugly with nothing relevant to add, lying in the infirmary jaundiced and sick as hell.

"Where we goin'," Josephine said.

"Campin'," Jackson replied.

"Huh?" Josephine said.

"Do I stutter?" Jackson said.

"Aren't we missin' somethin'?" she said.

"No."

"Like...you know...*food?*"

"Got it covered."

Without further ado, Peter pulled into the IGA store on 63rd and Alki. They piled out, Jackson jumping onto a shopping cart and coasting all the way into the store, emerging minutes later with crispy fried chicken, Lay's potato chips, cigarettes, and two gallons of Bali Hai wine. They were set.

Caitlin got over her shyness by the time they'd parked and hiked into Denny Creek up on Snoqualmie Pass and Jackson and Josephine had disappeared discreetly into the woods but no so discreet that Peter and Caitlin couldn't hear the moaning and screaming and bustling of soft earth and crushing Pine cones.

All the while embarrassed Caitlin tried to talk over this about her dear brother, whom she worried about, since he was a Green Beret who'd been AWOL two months now—in other words—he'd become an official deserter from the United States Army after thirty days. Peter shrugged that off, and knew he'd be okay, 'cause he was Jackson. "Jacky will be okay."

"Yeah, yeah, Jacky will be okay. Jacky's always okay."

"He just needs to turn himself in."

"But when will that be?"

"Mahn-*yahna*," Peter said. "He says mahn-*yahna*."

"Yeah, he's always saying mahn-*yahna*. Every day it's mahn-*yahna*..." They laughed and toked up some more and drank more Bali-hai wine and built a fire—and Jackson and Josephine returned all stoned and sated, arms around each other, tails wagging like happy puppies.

4

TWO

Now it just so happens that at this particular time in our history Peter Placik and his roommate Michael Hale were in the midst of a contest. Peter had entered the month depressed and in no particular mood for it, but now had entered a manic stage and was up to the ready. It had occurred to Peter and Michael that they were everywhere, gorgeous, bright, and full of promise and sexual freedom; exquisite and delightful, plump and healthy—and furthermore—available. It was 1968 after all, the height of the "hippie" movement, and Michael and Peter were riding its crest with various experimental drugs, psychedelic music, and unruly sex—the later of which they were both taking full advantage.

Five days into their contest they were tied at five hippie chicks apiece. On the sixth day Peter was about to take the lead with a girl he met that day on Alki Beach, upstairs in his room with her, sharing a joint when just then Julia (one of the two steady girlfriends Peter had at the time) announced herself at the door. Michael yelled up at him like the asshole he was that she was there, instead of telling her that Peter wasn't home, as Peter would have done for Michael, for crissakes.

Peter handed the joint to the girl and asked her to wait a moment, he'll be right back, sliding down the banister, legs up in a 90 degree arc like on parallel bars, to greet Julia, asking *her* to wait a moment, rushing back upstairs three steps at a time to quickly have his way with the flower girl who couldn't have been sixteen if she were a minute, then out the back door you go with a quick goodbye peck on the lips and a prodding slap on the tight little butt, then

5

rushing back to Julia—all the while asshole Michael is rolling around on the sofa grabbing his gut in hysterics, to the bafflement of Julia.

So Peter was up to six at this point and rushed Julia upstairs to make it seven. Everywhere it was rush here and rush there manically, like a Marx Brothers movie, hardly able too keep pace with himself. The next day Michael's girlfriend Karen was over, and Michael said he was going to the store—did anyone want anything? Karen said a pack of Marlboros, Peter said Camel straights, and Michael said, "Buy your own cancer sticks," slamming the door, since he didn't smoke cigarettes and wasn't about to enable their dastardly habit.

As soon as Michael slammed the door, it was instantly onto the carpet with Karen who'd been giving him the eye since day one. When Michael returned they were sitting on the sofa exactly where he'd left them, sharing a joint. Michael sniffed the air suspiciously and glared at them, Peter and Karen looking back innocently. Peter didn't feel too guilty about this since he figured Michael would have done the same given the chance: All's fair in fuck and fight.

They were on the honor system, however, and when the next day Michael said he was up to six, Peter said eight, and Michael said, "When'd that happen?" To save his honor Peter said, "While you were busy with your mother." Michael had brought some ancient pseudo hippie into their home that had to be on the dark side of forty.

Julia, and Peter's other girlfriend, Christine, bored him, but bored him inexplicably, since he could admit to nothing specific that should render boredom. Julia was a typical hippie chick, with no make-up applied or needed, with sad brown eyes and thick curly hair flailing out the breadth of her back. She was a recovering Catholic and converted Buddhist, and reading the poetry of Gary Snyder and Jack Kerouac, which had impressed Peter since he respected both writers immensely, believing *On the Road* to be the greatest generational novel since *The Catcher in the Rye*.

Christine, on the other hand, had difficulty comprehending the morning newspaper. She was just four inches short of Peter's six-foot-two with a slight slant in her mesmerizing cobalt blue eyes, lean physique, small *magnifico!* breasts, and a remarkable similarity to the actress Charlotte Rampling. She also happened to be married.

Nonetheless, on July 16 he made it sixteen with Jackson's sister Caitlin, and Michael and Peter were tied again. But unfortunately, this ended the contest for Peter. For a "virgin" (Jackson had said so about his sister), Caitlin took to sex like a flounder to H2O. The sex with her became so enamoring he had sex with her only, until the 31st. One day they had five orgasms each—the fifth simultaneous and finally suitably.

Caitlin had the face, freckles, and startling blue eyes of Liv Ulmann, the Swedish actress; and the body of Dolly Parton, the country singer, with small hips and *beaucoup* breasts perched taut behind thin, summer white see-through blouses. She became irresistible to Peter's manic young self, and the more they made love the more he inexplicably lusted for her, the unfortunate consequence of which was that by the 31st Michael's lead was virtually insurmountable, twenty to fourteen. Like a student cramming the night before a test, Peter made a ludicrous last-ditch effort to catch up, but managed only two more. He had been with Caitlin that morning as well, and when he had left abruptly to troll Alki, she later queried him as to where he had disappeared to—not so much checking up on him as simply curious, since they had been spending practically every minute together up to this point.

THREE

The four of them became a fixture on Alki Beach that summer, Peter reacting to Caitlin as if it were predestined they spend the rest of their lives together. He couldn't decipher exactly what it was he liked about her. It was simply as if they had been together, and would always be together, "soul-mates," as it were.

Caitlin buried the heartbreak of Eva. Eva and he had been a couple for eight months and he had been relatively faithful to her when he had left for basic training. The plan was to get married when he got out. They wrote to each other regularly and saw each other while he was on leave, unaware that while he was gone she was hanging out was with Dave Mathew. When he discovered this, it not only broke his heart and sent him into a deep suicidal depression, it facilitated his shell shock.

To make matters worse, Dave Mathew had been a good friend, and Peter had admired him for his James Dean looks and his magic behind the wheel of a car like Dean Moriarty, one day driving around with him all day in his '51 Chevy coup without breaks. He slammed the brake pedal up and down laughing like a mad man as he squirreled around objects and down-shifted to stops. He married someone and their baby had died under vague circumstances and then they had divorced.

And then it seemed, had his way with Peter's girlfriend while he was in Nam.

So he hadn't completely gotten over her by the time he met Caiti. And again, he didn't really know what he saw in her. It was a head scratcher.

It was October now, snapping south winds blew slanting rain—bullets. There wasn't much to do but keep the fire going with the wood he was stealing from Alki Beach and boink away the day and night.

"What is it about this obligation to adulthood," he said to Caiti philosophically one day all toked up in bed, his hands behind his head, Caitlin in a post-orgasmic half slumber, her head on his black, hairy chest, "and at the same time this repression of sexuality? We stifle our sexuality with guilt. Pleasure becomes depressed, nature confused."

Caitlin half opened her eyes and stared at her new boyfriend in wonder. She loved staring at him; she could stare at him all day and pretty much did; with his thick, brown, almost black hair; his long, thick eyelashes shading dreamy eyes nearly as black; his classic thick mustache, his long perfect nose and defined features. He looked even taller than he was, with his long dangling arms and huge hands. He was the best looking of all Jacky's friends.

"'Gatsby, who represented everything for which I had an unaffected scorn. If personality is an unbroken series of unaffected gestures, then there was something gorgeous about him, some heightened sensibility to the promises of life.' Let's see, I forget the next part… 'it was an extraordinary gift for hope, a romantic readiness such as I have never found in any other person and which it is not likely I shall ever find again. No—Gatsby turned out all right at the end, it was what preyed on Gatsby, what foul dust floated in the wake of his dreams that temporarily closed out my interest in the abortive sorrows and short-winded elations of men.'"

"What's a 'Gatsby'?" Caitlin said.

"*The Great Gatsby*. Only one of the towering novels in literature…I would give anything to be able to write like that."

"Maybe you will."

"I'll write, but I'll never be able to write like that."

Peter smoked his cigarette and pondered life while stoned out of his noggin.

They got up to wash, and then they made love again.

Peter liked his lovemaking neat and clean, always had. He was not perverse; he could be overly meticulous. He ejaculated *into*, not all over—if he could help it; into vaginas, tissue, eight feet into the atmosphere. He had been with someone just the other day, and nearing the climactic moment, she had said:

"Don't come inside of me," so he was compelled to leave a puddle in her navel. But most women these days had that issue taken care of with "The Pill". Into was tidy and orderly, the way he needed his life to be. All over was messy and disorderly, disturbing his conscious craving for conformity. In this way, he was a staunch conservative. He washed thoroughly before and after, and insisted on his partner doing the same. In this way, disease and infection were avoided.

When he was living at the Insane Hotel with Jackson McMahon, Johnny Hogan, Michael Hale and a constant parade of who knows who—a Holly hung about and infected everyone with gonorrhea—except Peter—and only because—he believed—he had insisted on this ritual of thorough bathing before and after. Unlike most others of this grungy hippie generation, he bathed daily—sometimes twice.

In Vietnam he contacted crabs somewhere, and the little buggers literally made him nauseated. The very thought of these black hideous little monsters subsisting on his flesh was repulsive. It didn't help that the Placik men were hairy as apes. His chest and groin were riddled with them. At the infirmary they shaved his body, including his groin area, and made him bathe with DDT.

FOUR

Jackson had written from Vancouver, B.C., where he had recently fled, since he was still a deserter. He felt free at last, free at last; no longer looking over his shoulder at every turn. The natives were friendly, the chicks were lovely, the air was brisk and clean, and best of all: he had a job! on a fishing boat making five bucks an hour. He told Peter he could get him a job there too if he wanted.

Peter had been thinking it over and decided to go. He explained to Caitlin how his last GI check had been cashed and he was broke. He needed a job. She nodded sadly as if he was leaving for good. And he didn't know that he wasn't.

He packed the V-dub van and left, unknowingly leaving behind a pregnant Caitlin.

———

He'd never worked harder in his life, 16-hour days, 7-day weeks. And the crew was as if split in half, with one half older redneck fishermen in their forties who'd been fishing all their lives, their bodies hardened and weathered from sun and salt sea winds, and suddenly there were these fucking hippie punks showing up on the boat, such as Peter and Jackson with hair down to their assholes just learning the trade and unable to keep up. Miller in particular kept harassing five-foot-six Jackson like the bully he was, calling Jackson a "hippie pussy." The guy was six-foot-four and built like the rugby player he was in the off-season, with thick shoulders wide as a doorway and legs like tree trunks from hauling in fish one way and pushing at rugby opponents the other for twenty years or more.

"I'm sick of you hippie pussies not keepin' up," he kept complaining, looking at Jackson.

Jackson said nothing. What was he to say to a forty-year-old redneck Canuck bonehead?

"Aye!" he nudged Jackson. "Ya hear me?"

Jackson continued to ignore him, busy working.

"Leave him alone," Peter said.

The crew stopped working a moment to observe this phenomenon. Nobody talked back to Miller.

"What?" Miller said.

"If you want to bully someone, bully me," Peter said.

When Peter was a boy his six-foot-four athletic father who might have been a quarterback in the NFL in a later era got tired of seeing his son coming home from school with purpled eyes and a bruised body and arrived home one day with a heavy bag and a speed bag and hung them from the joists in the basement and commenced to teach his oldest son how to fight. Every night he and dad would punch the bags, spar, and pound out pushups on the cold cement.

He instructed Peter the correct way to throw a punch, short erect jabs "from your toes" putting your whole body into it, and keeping the arms up, always protecting face and body.

Nowadays there was Mohammed Ali who danced the ring with his arms down, but Mohammed Ali was Mohammed Ali, one of a kind, putting the invincible Sonny Liston of all people on the canvas with a "phantom punch." Only in slow motion could you see Liston's head snapping and bobbing before he crumpled to the canvas, out.

Peter and Dad watched the Wednesday and Friday night fights studying the different styles but paying special attention to Sugar Ray Robinson, in his twilight fighting years now but still "pound for pound, the greatest fighter of all time." He still danced the ring like on a cloud, as graceful as a ballet dancer, as beautiful as a movie star, his face still smooth and unblemished, unlike Carmen Basilio who ducked and bored in like a bull, unrelenting, taking punches as defensively as their bags in the basement, his nose pounded flat, his face bulging with knots, his eyes slits buried behind layered waves of scar tissue.

Dad took away Peter's beloved Dickens and Twain and introduced him to Jack London and Ernest Hemingway. "No more of that sissy David Copperfield crap for you!"

At school, Warren Renfro, who liked to punch unsuspecting boys in the face or stomach, now stood before him like a statue, as if Peter were in his way. His fist looked fragile and in slow motion as it seemed to float through the air in a haymaker's arc, and Peter had all the time in the world. An uppercut caught Renfro's chin. His head snapped back and he stumbled backwards, asshole up in the air, landing square on his tail bone. He stared up at Peter in astonishment.

And so Peter developed a reputation at school, his body filling in with lean reeds of muscle from all the pushups and sit-ups and chin-ups from the steel bar dad had erected in the back yard between two four-by-fours cased in cement. No more coming home with purpled eyes and bruised body.

So when Miller approached Peter, it was an involuntary response. In high school, Peter had been known for power and speed. "The first thing ya try," Dad had said, "is a quick right. That usually ends it." And it struck true, smack dab on the nose, and Miller went down, and out. Miller would discover shreds of cartilage in his nose when he came to which would eventually have to be surgically removed.

Peter knelt down and picked the 220 pounds of Miller up and was about to toss him overboard until the others stopped him.

Miller left Jackson alone after that.

But the two friends wearied of the work and quit.

They hung around B.C. with the other hippies, panhandling for their daily bread. Jackson was a natural; people just handed over spare change to him like there was a pipeline to his paws. Peter looked on incredulously at whatever skill this entailed, but couldn't copy it. This unnatural skill paid the rent and bought the pot.

One afternoon, broke, they decided to stop at a bar and put their last quarter into a pool table. Jackson racked up the balls like he was Minnesota Fats, and their opponents scrutinized Peter as if he was Fast Eddie. All the while Peter wondered what Jackson was up to now: They couldn't play pool worth shit.

One of the opponents knocked in three balls on the break—two stripes and a solid. Then he nonchalantly proceeded to shoot, without taking time to think, putting in three more big ones before missing.

Peter realized their quarter wasn't going far.

Jackson spent a long moment observing the balls, as if calculating with algebraic precision how he was going to run the table, and then when finally deciding to shoot what was obviously the only shot available—the one ball in the corner pocket—he miscued and missed, sending the cue ball off into the other corner pocket for a scratch.

"What the fuck!" he exclaimed, standing over the table in disbelief. "How the fuck that happen?" he said to Peter, who shrugged back at him.

Their opponents peeked at each other and smiled.

The other opponent stood and took his turn. He put away two more stripes and their only ball left was the eight ball. But it was a difficult shot. All those little ones on the table were in his way, and he was going to have to bank it into a corner pocket, which he did, without concentrating, and it went in followed by the cue ball for a scratch on the eight ball.

So Pete and Jackson won without Peter taking a shot.

"Tough luck, guys," Jackson said.

"Go again?" one of them said, on his haunches putting in another quarter.

"Why not?" Jackson said. "But whataysay we make this one a little more interesting?"

The one racking up the balls paused in what he was doing and looked up at Jackson suspiciously. "How interesting?"

Jackson shrugged. "I dunno…Say…Five bucks a head?"

Peter wondered what the hell he was doing. Neither of them was any good at pool, and he was challenging two dudes who obviously had spent some time around a pool table for ten bucks that they didn't have.

Peter looked at their opponents, who were actually discussing the challenge as if Peter and Jackson might actually be good.

Peter leaned into Jackson who was standing at the table ready to break.

"What are you doing?" he whispered.

"Don't worry."

"They're *good*," Peter said

"We'll win." He shrugged as if a win was preordained by providence.

"We *have* to win," Peter said, stating the obvious.

"That's right. We *have* to win."

"Look at those dudes, Jacky. They're not only good pool players; they look like they could be defensive linemen for the B.C. Lions."

"But we got you." He smiled.

"You're nuts."

"We'll win." He shrugged. "We won the last one, didn't we?"

"That was luck! They weren't even concentrating and practically ran the table before I even had a shot!"

"I just have a feeling this is our lucky day, Peter. Here." He handed Peter the cue stick. "You break."

"I'll break it over your head." Peter grabbed the cue stick.

The balls were racked. Their opponents had accepted the challenge. Pete broke, and the one ball went into the side pocket.

Peter studied the position of the balls and decided on the three ball in the corner pocket.

It went in.

"Good shot, Peter!" Jackson said, encouragingly.

Peter gave him a dirty look.

The cue ball had rolled into the opposite side of the table as if it had a mind of its own, leaving Peter with absolutely nothing to shoot at.

He hit it softly, dislodging a cluster of balls. None went in.

Peter and Jackson watched in awe as their opponent proceeded to knock in one stripe after another, this time taking the game quite seriously, and Peter's heart began to beat like a hammer as he realized that this guy was already thinking about a few extra bucks of beer money.

All the guy had left was the eight ball. Peter peered at Jackson, and Jackson appeared as calm and confident as a con man, as if they still had a chance, as if just because they *had* to win it was predestined that they would. The only problem that Peter could ascertain was that their opponents were not aware of this particular mandate.

The man leaned at the table and studied the shot like a golf pro. He slowly approached the cue ball, watched it like a cat prowling prey as he slowly and meticulously chocked his cue stick. He bent over the ball slowly prepared to shoot.

Suddenly, Jackson split. Peter turned and spotted his little legs spinning like a cartoon up the stairs that led to the exit, coat tucked securely into his torso like he was carrying a football for yardage.

Peter cast a quick glance at their opponents. They appeared confused. "What the fuck?" one enquired of Peter.

Peter did not answer.

Jackson's short stubby legs were no match for Peter's long lean ones, and he passed Jackson half way down the street.

"Wait for me!" Jackson screamed, but Peter ignored him. He would wait for Jackson the way Jackson had waited for him.

"Peter!" Jackson screamed. "Help!"

Peter glanced over his shoulder and saw that the Canuck pool players had grabbed onto Jackson and were flinging him about like the squirming little squirrel that he was.

Peter wondered what to do. Naturally he wasn't crazy about the idea of going back there and having to deal with about 500 pounds of Canadian bacon. But he didn't want to leave his best friend in dire jeopardy either.

He reluctantly decided to go back and attempt to diplomatically explain their embarrassing predicament, hoping that they would be somewhat sympathetic and not have to fight one another over twenty lousy bucks.

"Where's our money?" one of them bellowed, shaking Jackson like an eighty pound pit bull with an eight pound Yorkie.

Jackson waved a trembling finger Peter's way. "He's got it!" he screamed hysterically.

They tossed Jackson aside like the rat he was and made for Peter.

Peter had run track in high school and was the fastest in the school in the 100-yard-dash, clocking in a 10.2. He knew it was doubtful that they could catch him. Nonetheless, he ran like never before. It was the longest sprint of his life. He never looked back. He dodged pedestrians like he was on a football field. He vaulted a garbage receptacle like a track hurdle. He sidestepped a German shepherd that had lunged at him. He tip-toed it over a parked vehicle like on thin ice. He sprinted between buildings and through alleyways, until finally he could sprint no more, and he braked to a halt hands on bent knees through spasms of laughter, his lungs on fire like the time he was tear-gassed on Alki by the pigs. He could go no farther.

———

When he got back to the apartment he found Jackson on the sofa with shoes off and feet propped up on the coffee table watching Canadian football on TV. He was toking on a joint and sipping a beer.

"Hey, Peter," he said dismissively, like it was just another day.

"WHAT THE FUCK!" Peter screamed at him.

Jackson jumped up. "Peter! Hey, man! Here, sit down, man! I'll get ya a beer!"

Jackson was infuriatingly snug and content, cool and relaxed, as if nothing in the world could possibly ever be wrong.

"What in the *FUCK* are you *DOING!*" Peter said to him, barely able to maintain his composure.

"What's wrong?"

"What's *WRONG?* You almost got us killed, you *FUCK!*"

"Peter, Peter, Peter." He shook his head admonishingly. "I knew you could outrun those fat clods. You think I woulda done what I done otherwise?"

Peter stared at him, seething, at a loss for words.

"If I had let you come back to me, they mighta beat the shit out of both of us, man."

Peter realized this was likely so.

"They quit chasing you after a block, man."

Peter dipped his shoulders and collapsed on the sofa. "They did?"

"Fuck, yes. And they were winded. You were way gone by then. How far you run for crissakes?"

Jackson laughed. "I'll get you a beer."

Peter laughed back. He had to admit, it was kind of funny.

FIVE

A few days later, close to midnight Peter was reclined on the sofa, a beer on the coffee table, reading Kafka's *The Trial*, when Jackson came bursting through the front door. There was nothing unusual about this other than the fact that he was naked.

"Peter! You wouldn't believe what just happened!"

"Jackson—how could I not believe anything you have to say—after this." He gestured to Jackson's tight little, muscle-laden body.

Jackson went into his room and emerged a moment later pulling clothes on this way and that. "I met this chick in a bar," he began.

"Uh huh."

"It prob'ly wouldn't a mattered none if she'd told me she was hooked up, but she didn't."

"Uh huh."

"We were goin' at it like gangbusters when we heard the front door slam. The bitch panicked. She told me to get into the closet, but before I could do that, the bedroom door flew open, and there's this dude about six-eight and 300 pounds filling the doorway, staring at us in a drunken rage."

"Six-eight?"

"At least. He was the biggest fucker I ever seen, I swear. He reached for a vase sittin' on the chest a' drawers next to him and flung it. I ducked and it smashed against the wall. Then he rushed at me, his huge arms out swingin' like bear claws, as if he would tear me limb from limb. I jumped off the bed, where he landed, collapsing the bed frame to the floor. I ran out of the bedroom, out the front door, and here I am."

Peter laughed.

"It ain't funny, man."

"Why didn't you take the bus?"

"Ha ha."

"How many people saw you running down the street stark raving naked?"

"Ya know, Peter, I didn't take the time to count."

Pete kept laughing.

"We gotta go back there."

"What for?"

"For my clothes and my wallet, my ID, all my money n' shit."

"Six-eight, you say?"

"Maybe only six-six…Those are my best suit of goin' out duds, man. An' I paid fifty bucks for them leather cowboy boots."

———

They knocked on the door. A moment later a young brunette answered. When she opened the door wide they could see this giant of a man sitting on the sofa with his hands in his face, sobbing. "*Fucking bitch!*" he wailed at Peter and Jackson for commiseration. "*Goddam fuckin' bitch!*"

A roaring fire was going in the fireplace. In the midst of it was Jackson's boots and clothes 'n shit.

SIX

Peter had had it. He had gone into the kitchen after cleaning it spotless not half an hour earlier to find a banana peeling in the sink, the ice tray out with ice melting, bread out on the table unwrapped, peanut butter out with the cap off, and bread crumbs littering the counter and floor.

He stormed into the living room where Jackson was eating a peanut butter/banana sandwich watching a football game, and let it rip: He yelled that Jackson was "lazy, unkempt, ignorant, sloppy, and inconsiderate."

Jackson stopped chewing and stared back at Peter incredulously. "Unkempt?"

"I've had it, Jacky. I can't take your shit any longer."

"*What* shit!"

"I just cleaned up the kitchen not half an hour ago, and it's a mess again!"

"Well *shit*, man, I was gonna clean up after I ate, but *shit*, man." He jumped up and marched into the kitchen. He threw his half eaten sandwich in the garbage. He started cleaning up.

Peter watched, arms crossed.

"What you said in there really hurt, man. 'specially the part 'bout bein' ignorant." He tossed the banana peeling at the garbage can. It slapped the side of the garbage can and slid like a snake to the floor. Peter picked it up and dropped it in.

Peter went to the refrigerator for a beer.

"Just 'cause I never finished high school."

"I didn't mean to call you ignorant."

"But I am ignorant, and that's what really hurts. I know I'm not perfect, Peter, but you ain't exactly without fault yourself, ya know."

"I know."

"As long as we're bein' so open 'n shit, there's a few things I could say 'bout you, too."

"Like what?"

"Like the way you talk—for one."

"The way I talk?"

"You're always using big words."

"I am?"

"Yeah, big motherfucking words nobody who hasn't had about twenty years of college can understand." He spread his little arms out like wings. "An' the books you read. Russian novels a thousand pages thick like that Gagol dude or whatever, Dusty...Dos..."

"Dostoyevsky."

"See what I mean? Who reads that shit much less know how to pronounce the names?"

"Dostoyevsky is easy reading. Joyce is hard."

"Joyce who?"

"James Joyce. He wrote *Ulysses.*"

"I saw the movie...No wait...That was *Hercules.*"

"And *Finnegan's Wake.* Now that's difficult reading."

"There you go again showing how smart you are. Just because you read Russian novels don't make you a genius, you know."

"I know."

"An' 'nother thing, you're too damn fussy about the way the place looks. Every time I have a smoke you're washing out the ash tray. It's really annoying."

"I suppose I am a bit obsessive compulsive."

"I don't know what that means either but if it means you're an asshole, then I guess you're obsessive compulsive."

Peter stared at Jackson guiltily, hardly able to believe his friend could say such mean things to him. "I can't help the way I am."

"What makes you think I can?"

Peter stared at him thoughtfully. He had never considered the possibility that Jackson *couldn't* change. Maybe he was lazy and irresponsible and a deserter from the United States Army because it was inherent in his personality and there was nothing he or anyone else could do about it, like being born gay or left-handed.

"All right," Peter conceded.

"Let's go get a beer."

Peter thought about all of Jackson's antics in the past that had infuriated him, and yet he still managed to get over it and forgive him. There was the time he borrowed one of Peter's shirts that was way too big for him and came home the next day wearing someone else's shirt that was way too small. And the time he borrowed Peter's 10-speed Peugeot bicycle and returned it with two flat tires and a broken fork. The time he loaned him his VW bug and it came home with the front bumper bashed in. The time he was riding with Jackson in a '55 Pontiac he had borrowed from someone else and it stalled on the I-90 floating bridge and they'd had to get out and hitchhike and listened on the radio in the car that picked them up that there was a stalled vehicle on the I-90 Bridge backing up traffic for miles. Was that all that simply part and parcel of the Jackson McMahon personality and there was nothing to be done about it?

At the tavern they gulped down a pitcher and ordered another. Jackson said: "I don' know why I said those things about you, I'm sorry."

"You said them because of what I said about you. Let's forget about it."

"Yeah, but what I said about you really aren't faults. They may be annoying as hell, but reading Russian novels can hardly be considered a fault. I don't get how they could be entertaining, but to each his own...I'm the one with the bad habits, and I'll try to get better, Peter, I really will. They've gotten me into one jam after another."

Peter stared into his schooner and said: "And I'll try and not be so ostentatious in my conversation in the future."

Jackson looked at him. "Austin who?"

"Ostentatious...Didactic...Doctrinaire...Erudite..."

"Peter, I don't know what any of those words mean."

"Pompous? Stilted?"

Jackson shrugged, shook his head, and sighed.

"An asshole in the way I talk?"

"Ah."

They sipped their beer and marveled at the humungous breasts on the barmaid.

"I got a 'Dear Jackie' letter from Josie yesterday."

"I didn't know you and Josephine still had a thing going."

"I would marry that woman, Peter."

"No shit. Then why don't you?"

"I need to get unfucked first."

Peter nodded empathetically and drained his beer, gesturing for two more.

"And I got a letter from Cait. She keeps asking about you."

Peter shrugged.

"You broke my sister's heart, buddy."

Peter said nothing, and Jackson said: "She's going to marry a lawyer."

Peter looked at Jackson in alarm. "Who is?"

Jackson stared back and laughed. "You're hung up on her, admit it...But no, Josie."

Peter looked away, shoulders relaxing.

"I can't blame her," he went on. "A lawyer for crissakes. What do I have to offer her? I want to settle down like any other normal asshole. Get married, have kids, but a house...you know, the whole American dream bullshit."

"'America is a myth, an abstract idea.'"

"Huh?"

"Henry Miller said that."

"I don't know any Henry Miller."

"He wrote *Tropic of Cancer*, among many other great books."

"Now there's a book I've read...at least the good parts."

"It would appear that both our lives appear less than auspicious at the moment."

"There you go again."

"What?"

"'Auspicious'. What the fuck that mean?"

"It means propitious."

"Jesus Christ, Peter!"

"Favorable, hopeful, fruitful, optimistic."

"Why didn't you just say so?"

"Anyway, I wouldn't worry if I were you. I'm sure your talents will see you through. You've gotten by so far, haven't you?"

"Getting by. It's the story of my life."

"It's the story of most people's lives. 'The mass of men lead lives of quiet desperation.'"

Jackson glared at him.

"Thoreau."

Jackson shook his head and sighed. "You, on the other hand, are hopeless...But look at Josie. She *loved* me, man, she really did. But she's going to marry a *lawyer*, for crissakes. Now you tell me, who's more likely to provide a stable life for her? Me, an army deserter with no job or future prospects... or an established lawyer who will prob'ly be a millionaire someday?"

"You?"

"You're *such* an asshole."

They both laughed, the beer going down like water now, the ugly barmaid with the big tits looking better by the schooner.

Then the stimulus turned to depression, and they stared sullenly into their schooners for awhile. Suddenly Peter was missing Caiti. He started thinking about his own life, how nothing was proceeding forward. He could be on the GI bill, getting his sorry ass back to school. It suddenly seemed time to finish sowing his wild oats.

"Are you planning on staying here?" Peter said.

"Here?" Jackson pointed at the bar. "At the tavern?"

"No." He laughed. "In B.C."

He shrugged. "I don't know. I don't know nothin'. An' don't tell me I used a double negative."

"There's nothing up here for me. I'm heading back to Seattle."

"How 'bout north to Alaska? We could get on another fishing boat. Or here in Canada, working on the pipeline? We'll make a fortune."

"I don't think so. It's back to Seattle for me."

Then Jackson nodded solemnly, as if it were finally time to do something about his own status. "Yeah...me too...I suppose."

And in the morning Peter opened his eyes to one of the ugliest women he had ever been with, but ugly in an interesting way, interesting like an ordinary face rendered interesting with a six inch scar down the cheek.

SEVEN

When Peter was two-years-old, his pregnant mother would wheel him around the Safeway store in the grocery cart. Astonished shoppers would see Peter point at the cereal boxes and say: "Wheaties! Cheerios! Grape Nuts! Corn Flakes!"

"Can he *read?*" someone would remark to Peter's mother in astonishment, and she would shrug back, not knowing whether Peter could read or that he had memorized the cereal boxes from TV commercials.

In this regard he was considered precocious. However, sometimes Peter would blank out and just sit and stare for several minutes and nothing anyone did caught his attention.

They decided to keep Peter out of kindergarten for "emotional reasons," and on his first day of first grade he stood on the steps of the front door of the classroom and waited for the class to start, not wanting to be late. Next thing he knew he was still standing out on the step alone and the class was full of pupils.

These lapses in consciousness would occur infrequently throughout Peter's life.

When Peter was eleven his brother Paul was born, in 1959. Paul would grow up tall and handsome like his two brothers Peter and Perry. He would be thicker with more natural musculature than Peter or Perry, more athletic than either, a soccer player—though he would have excelled at any sport. His legs were like oak trunks, bulging with unnatural muscles that Peter and Perry lacked. He would someday be a cabinet maker, like his father and grandfather, fascinated with the handmade skills of his grandfather Otto, who had craftsmen skills with wood

29

that would become a lost art, skills that he had brought over from Poland having learned them from his father. He made ornate cedar chests with inlays without a rotor, antique style roll-top desks that he stained in an Arts and Crafts style. Paul hung around his grandfather throughout his childhood, and Otto taught Paul how to hand carve dovetail joints so tight they didn't need glue. Their grandfather was ahead of his time in the fifties and sixties and never made much money, but Paul would take advantage of the Arts and Crafts renaissance of the eighties and nineties and become well known for his custom made cabinets and Stickley-like replicas and become wealthy from it. Through all this time he would continue to play soccer and lift weights and be a six-foot-three-inch enforcer on the soccer field, fearsome and feared—and constantly yellow carded and red carded. Unlike his brothers, Paul would become prematurely bald while just in his twenties, just like his six-foot-one inch, 220 pound grandfather had in his youth, who had been considered pound for pound just about the toughest immigrant around in a district predominant with oversized Scandinavians.

If the three brothers had bothered to take an IQ test, Paul would undoubtedly have had the highest score. Nevertheless, Paul would become a cabinet maker, Perry would be an architect, and Peter would become a professor of English Literature at the University of Washington, where unavoidable flings with co-ends would render him in perennial trouble.

One year before Paul was born, when Peter was ten, he fell madly in love with a neighbor girl who was fourteen.

The love that Peter had for Judy is integral to this history because it was a love that would become unequaled and have profound psychological impact on our hero, affecting all future relationships. She was all he thought about night and day. His brief attention to other details in his life invariably brought his thoughts back to Judy. He lay in bed thinking about her each night unable to sleep, and she was the first thought that popped into his head when he woke in the morning. Interestingly, he never dreamt about her. Peter's dreams made absolutely no sense and had no relation to anything, far as he could tell. He was so in love with her he couldn't eat; eating made him sick to his stomach. His was a classic case. To Peter, Judy was the ultimate in sophistication, maturity, and beauty; a Venus goddess no less.

She had a younger sister by the name of Collette who was eleven and in love with Peter. Peter knew this because she told him. She said so out of the blue one day when they were sitting on the front steps at Peter's house. "I love you," she repeated, when Peter hadn't responded. Peter was embarrassed, and now confused. Peter loved Judy. Collette loved Peter. Did love always make no sense like this? Peter pondered.

One day Judy was sitting cross-legged on the grass whittling a piece of wood with her ever sharp jackknife, and Peter stared hypnotized at the top of her silky brown hair, strands of sun bleach gleaming in the sun. He bent down and brushed the top of her sweetly perspiring head with his trembling lips.

She stared back at him in open-mouthed disbelief.

The very next day Peter sat in Judy and Collette's living room reading a classics comic book (*Treasure Island*) when Collette marched through the living room naked, giggling. Judy gasped, quickly covered Peter's eyes and politely told him he had better leave.

She was the epitome of good and right and proper.

So this summer passed and Peter's passion only grew. He would wonder how he could possibly love her more than he did, and then he would. He wouldn't see how he could possibly go on living without her in his life.

One day Peter looked out his front window and saw his beloved walking by the house with Arthur Paulguin, who lived down the street. Arthur was Peter's age, but had been held back a year. His curiosity compelled him to follow them, which led to the wooded ravine one block from Peter's house. Judy, Collette, Peter and Perry spent much of their summer there playing in these woods. They had carved paths through the thick brush and blackberry vines with a machete. They had built a wooden platform out of plywood and two by fours for private club meetings. It was their private sanctuary from the nonsense of other children. No one else was allowed there.

Until now: now Judy had brought Arthur Paulguin here, who was prematurely pubescent, looking older than his age, his voice cracking, his upper lip sprouting blondish wisps of hair, blond and blue-eyed handsome, combing his hair in a ducktail like a teenage greaser.

Peter hid behind a fir tree and observed in horror and disbelief as they climbed the maple tree to the platform and sat next to each other with their legs swaying and kissing each other.

Peter ran home in tears. This betrayal was more than he could bear. He wanted to die. He hated her. He loved her so much he plotted how to kill her and keep her forever. He couldn't put this absolute horror out of his mind and now hated her more than he had ever hated anybody or anything. What was one to do with such a horrific love?

When he was thirteen he lost his virginity to Collette, and subsequently avoided here like the plague.

By the age of fourteen Peter, Arthur Paulguin, and Gordon Inman were best friends. Arthur had towered over Peter and Gordon, but now Peter and Gordon began to sprout, so that by sixteen Peter was six-foot-two and Gordon was six-foot-three while Arthur remained a solid five-foot-eleven. The three handsome young men developed their muscles at the West Seattle YMCA. All three were athletically gifted, but Gordon excelled, and in high school was the starting quarterback of the football team. Gordy's bright ringlets of blond hair were seldom combed or washed, and despite dressing sloppily in the same pair of Levi's and white t-shirt, he always managed to look good. The three of them strutted the halls of West Seattle High with friendly, sparkly-eyed, white-toothed smiles, and the girls responded with shy gasps and goo-goo eyes.

After high school, Arthur would join the marines and be killed in Vietnam at the age of nineteen.

Gordy's wealthy parents would send him away to Harvard Law School, and this was the lawyer who was engaged to Josephine, until Gordy came home early from the office one day and found her in bed with Jackson McMahon.

EIGHT

Peter took the train home from B.C. to discover unexpectedly a pregnant Caitlin. He wasn't prepared for this responsibility. He'd had other plans.

"It's okay," Caitlin said calmly. "The baby and I will get along fine without you."

"Don't be ridiculous," he said. "We'll get an abortion."

Catholic Caitlin gasped. "I would never do that. Don't ever ask me to do that. Don't worry. I'm not going to burden you with this responsibility. We can take care of ourselves."

They got married by a justice of the peace. Jackson and Josephine stood as witnesses. At home they celebrated with a bong. Except for Caitlin; she wouldn't indulge.

"I don't want the baby stoned on that stuff," she explained.

They all looked at her totally nonplussed.

"What stuff?" Jackson said.

"Pot, speed, acid—any of that stuff."

Everyone continued to stare at her numb and stoned, toking away.

Jackson said to Peter: "I hear Perry is hanging out with smackers."

"Bullshit," Peter responded. "Perry would never do that."

But when Peter saw his younger brother, he recognized the symptoms, the slotted glazed over eyes, the pin-point pupils, the scratching of his skin the color of chrome. He obviously had hepatitis.

When Peter and Perry were in high school he had discovered that Perry was smoking marijuana and dropping LSD. Peter threatened to kick his skinny

33

ass. The summer after Peter graduated he had joined his little brother smoking pot and dropping acid.

But this was different. Heroin was contrary to their grandiose visions of mind expansion, peace, love, and nirvana. It was decadent and evil. Smack simply would not do.

So Peter continued to abide in denial.

Until Perry got busted selling smack to a narc. He was tossed into a jail cell. The jailers laughed at him, writhing and sweating on the jail floor in inconceivable agony from withdrawals.

When he got out on bail he immediately went back on junk. When he was sentenced to two months in the King Country Jail he had to go through withdrawals again. This time when he got out he got counseling, and was prescribed methadone. He moved in with Peter and Caitlin, who were renting a tiny cottage on Alki Avenue.

Before the baby was born, Caitlin convinced Peter to quit smoking, pot as well as cigarettes. The pot was easy; the holes in his head began to heal. The cigarettes were another matter. A day didn't go by for a year when he wasn't tempted to light up. But he didn't. He never smoked another cigarette again. Pot was another matter.

He became astounded at how clear his thoughts suddenly became, no longer foggy with weed. Enrolled at Seattle Community College, knowledge seeped into his brain like a sponge. He started getting As when before he had to study his ass off to get Bs and Cs. He even got a B in algebra, a requirement towards his degree.

Once a week, Perry hopped on the metro bus on his way downtown to cop his weekly allotment of methadone.

Peter started exercising again. He would go jogging, do pushups and sit-ups. He rigged a steel bar between the two apple trees in the front yard and did chin-ups. He shadow-boxed in the front room mirror.

Getting home from a leisurely jog one day, he told Perry he had run a mile.

"Bullshit," Perry replied. "Nobody could do that."

One winter's day there was a sudden snow storm. Snow was piling up so quickly that it took the city by surprise. Cars, trucks, and buses were turned sideways all over town. The buses quit running. Unfortunately, it was the day Perry needed to go downtown to fill his weekly prescription.

"The buses aren't running," Peter said.

"I'll have to walk then."

"In this storm? Don't be crazy. It must be eight miles over and back. Skip the shit this week."

Peter didn't understand the urgency. He watched Perry get all bundled up and leave.

Perry pushed through the storm like Doctor Zhivago across the frozen Russian tundra. Several hours later he returned with his weekly allotment.

NINE

Married now with a kid on the horizon, Peter decided it was time to settle down. In addition to his job at a local steel manufacturer, he was taking a shitload of classes and had started writing again. He hadn't done any real writing since high school, where the buxom blonde blue-eyed English teacher, Miss Groening, recognized a talent when she saw one and brought him home regularly for tutoring. They worked on more than his syntax. Peter was falling in love with her until he learned he was not the only one she brought home for after school extracurricular activities. He and Arthur compared notes.

After high school he had experimented with some scribbling, stoned out of his gourd thinking he was the reincarnation of Shakespeare, only to read it when straight and realize it was rubbish. But he had always thought of himself as a writer, even when he was in fourth grade when he was creating his own Edgar Rice Burroughs like adventures with his own heroic ape man. One day the teacher, Miss Willis, looked at what he was reading, which was *The Adventures of Tarzan*. She said this was too advanced for him. At home he told his mother what Miss Willis had said, and she got angry.

"Nonsense. Tomorrow you go back to class with this." She handed him *The Three Musketeers*.

"But I've already read it."

"That's all right. Great literature is always better the second time around."

The next day Miss Willis observed him reading Dumas's famous novel, and when the kids returned from recess she said: "Children, listen up. Peter is going to read for us. Come up here, Peter, and read your book to the class."

Peter did so, struggling only with certain names such as D'Artagnan. Miss Willis was flummoxed. *Why was he flunking out in mathematics? Why couldn't he do a simple thing like multiplying double digits? Why couldn't he complete a story problem? If he can read like this he isn't stupid...I know, she thought, he's not stupid he's lazy, a classic underachiever. Well, it will certainly be indicated in his grades. I will see to that!*

And now Peter decided to get serious. He would learn how to write. His schooling would be directed specifically towards this particular goal. He got up at 4:00 a.m. to drink coffee then do pushups and sit-ups before traipsing off to his job and then after work to school. He planned to write an epic novel about his experiences in Nam.

At work he became an apprentice sheet metal worker. A skill was necessary in case he needed a job that would pay decent wages. He struggled with it; especially the trigonometry part. But he did it. And of course exercise; pushups, sit-ups, and chin-ups on the bar he rigged outside. He jogged two or three miles every night. He took up tennis. He ate an apple and a banana every morning. He chomped on carrots, celery, and mixed nuts all day. It was all about discipline. He needed discipline to get through this. He would discipline himself like a Zen Buddhist monk—except for the celibacy part. Discipline was what writing was all about, after all. Sitting one's ass down and doing it; writing it down in longhand and revising it over and over until it was right and then typing it out with his Royal manual typewriter. One must do this. One must use one's senses and direct one's total energy toward one's specific goal.

Peter was 22, overflowing with unimaginable energy and idealistic ambition. It was boundless. He conducted his life in a manic-like fever. But then he would crash, exhausted and depressed.

In compensation for the decent wages he was making in a union shop, one potential sacrifice was to his health, which he risked breathing carcinogenic, rust-resistant, metal-grinding dust and welding fumes. Most of the older workers who had been in the industry a long time wheezed like emphysema sufferers. The physical state of these workers was appalling. Forty-year-old men looked sixty. Fifty-year old-men looked ready to die, but of course couldn't; they had families to feed. They couldn't breathe through their noses and were mostly deaf from decades of factory noise. In addition, most of them were heavy cigarette smokers and heavy drinkers; it seemed to come with the job. They ate funk food and swallowed huge thermoses of black coffee and reported to the pub promptly after work. They scoffed at respirators and ear protection and believed only in hard work and voting Republican. They never missed a day's work, regardless of how hungover they were. They refused to listen to anyone tell them that their working conditions were anything but exemplary. But all Peter could think about was Upton Sinclair's *The Jungle*. A carcinogenic white fog hovered on the factory floor. During break, Peter watched it settle the way fog dissipates in a noonday sun. Workers in the nitric acid tank where stainless steel parts were scrubbed and cleaned to a brilliant sheen inhaled hot nitric acid fumes. Toxic waste washed down the drain disappearing to who knows where, presumably Elliott Bay.

———

One day Jackson, Josie, and Perry were sitting and staring at Peter and Caitlin's baby boy, Thomas. Peter held his precious son in his lap delicately, like a piece of expensive china. They were all in awe that such a beautiful, toe-headed entity could come into existence.

Perry announced out of thin air: "That's it; I'm quitting methadone."

Peter, Caitlin, and Josie all smiled doubtfully. Jackson toked on a fresh joint, and nodded his head at Perry exuberantly, as if he understood completely.

Perry was again staying with Peter and Caitlin, and for the following month Perry suffered in unbelievable physical agony, but refused to go downtown to cop. He lay in bed shivering then sweating then vomiting—for one entire month. He couldn't eat. He couldn't sleep. He felt as if he had the Black Plague. He wanted to die; he prayed to God to let him die. But the month finally passed, and he emerged from his room one day, rail thin but rosy cheeked and asked for breakfast, declaring himself clean.

Peter was lacing up his Nike Trainers.

"Going for a run?" Perry said. "I'll join you."

"I'm going two miles."

"I'll tag along."

"You don't have running shoes."

"I'll run with these." He had on a pair of flat soled leather sandals.

"No way." Peter shook his head, adamant.

"Just a minute."

Perry disappeared into his room and reappeared with an old pair of beat up Converse All-stars.

"All right." Peter shrugged doubtfully. "*Vamonos.*"

They left. Peter took off in what Perry thought was a sprint, but was actually only seven minute miles. For two blocks Perry could barely keep up. He staggered to a halt.

"I'll see you back at the house," he said.

———

But Perry continued to go out with him every day. It wasn't too long before Perry was actually outrunning him.

Peter bought a new Motobecane ten-speed bicycle and began training on that. Perry followed suit, purchasing a used ten-speed Peugeot, and the pair were seen spinning all over West Seattle in the *Tour de Alki*.

Perry tagged along with Peter to the tennis courts on Alki. They were soon about even. Usually Peter won, but Perry was winning more and more. Then Perry took lessons from a club pro. Soon he was beating Peter handily in straight sets. Whatever activity Peter adopted, Perry followed suit and excelled, surpassing Peter's skill in running, biking, and tennis.

In school, Peter was getting mostly As. Perry got a job at the Post Office, enrolled in school and got straight As. In four years Perry got his bachelor's degree and Peter was in graduate school.

But we're getting ahead of ourselves. As soon as Perry moved out of Peter and Caitlin's house, Jackson moved in. He was still AWOL and running out of places to hide. But soon the MP's came sniffing around, and Jackson had to split again.

As soon as Jackson left, Peter started itching. Dropping his drawers, he saw that he had crabs! What the fuck! Where'd *they* come from! He took off his shirt and saw the hideous little buggers crawling through his chest hair! He rushed to the doc for a remedy. He had to shower several times a day with prescription lice shampoo and wash all the clothes and linen and bed covers in the house. He had the carpet scrubbed clean by professionals.

Looking in the medicine cabinet one day, he saw that there were two bottles of prescription lice shampoo instead of one. One was for him, and the other dated previously was for a Jackson McMahon.

TEN

Jackson finally got tired of running and turned himself in, expecting to be sentenced to the stockade for five years or more. Instead they promptly issued him a general discharge. There were so many deserters in this war—more deserters than any war in American history since the Civil War—that they just wanted them off the books and out of their hair.

He showed up at the house one day looking revitalized and healthy. The heavy burden of being a deserter for two years had been left behind somewhere in the complicated history of Jackson McMahon. He announced that he had a job at Stack Lumber, operating a crane.

"How'd you manage that?"

Peter had worked at Stack Lumber briefly, and knew that all new hires were put on the Green Chain, pulling lumber off and stacking it. Most didn't make it through the first day, the labor was so arduous. But if they could make it on the Green Chain they had a job—a good paying job, too, since it was union.

"I dunno. After a coupla days they put me up in a crane." Jackson shrugged.

Peter shook his head and Caitlin smiled, each aware of Jackson's rare talent at procuring a job as easily as tying a pair of shoe laces. The hard part for Jackson was *keeping* the job. But Jackson always managed to come out smelling like a rose regardless of what he did. It was beyond Peter's and most everybody else's comprehension.

Peter cracked open two Budweiser's. Jackson grabbed one and said: "I'd better go easy; I have to work tonight."

"Tonight?"

"Yeah, I'm on the graveyard shift. I love it. I work six hours and get paid for eight."

"When do you sleep?"

"Sleep? What's that?" He guzzled the beer and reached for another. "Hey, man, there's a party at Roach's."

"Yeah? But the V-dub's broke down."

"Bummer. We'll have to hitchhike."

They hiked up the Admiral Way hill to 35th, thumbs out, Jackson talking most of the way about his plans, which included him and Josephine getting married and buying a house out in the country somewhere away from the congestion and shit of the city where they would have a wood-burning stove and chickens and grow vegetables n' shit.

They got picked up by an old black man in an old white Cadillac. He had an unruly mass of tight salt and pepper curls on his head and a white mustache. There was a bottle of Jack Daniels in his lap, which he shared with Peter and Jackson. Jackson returned the favor by sharing a joint with the old man.

Jackson kept talking, and the old man kept listening, Jackson pausing long enough to say "Turn here, turn there," and in no time they had pulled up at the curb at Roach's.

"Thanks, brother!" Jackson said, handing back the bottle of Jack, along with two bennies for the road.

Inside Roach's (His name was John Roche, which of course became "Roach"), Peter saw some old friends he hadn't seen in a while since being busy with a family, work, and school. But they hadn't changed much other than for the most part the Love Generation had now brought alcohol into the mix of marijuana and other prescribed as well as non-prescribed recreational inebriants.

Roach was looking older than his 26 years, pot-bellied and balding, his face red and drawn. A new drug had also made its entrée into the recreational mix: cocaine. Peter had never tried it and wasn't about to now in his prescribed road of Buddhist enlightenment and meditation. He was reading Alan Watts and Soyen Shaku.

But he did crack open a beer; no point in being a fanatic about it.

Massell was there. He had been in Nam with Peter and talked about nothing else: He was going to write a book about his experiences. Everybody was going to write a book about their experiences in Vietnam, but so far no one had, as far as Peter knew.

Johnny Hogan was there. Peter still saw him around on occasion, usually falling ass down shit-faced drunk. His alcoholism was a new hot topic of discussion, especially among those who were in denial about their own particular issues with booze.

And the Fladabo's were there: Big Flad and Little Flad. Little Flad at six-foot-three was actually two inches taller than Big Flad, who was the big brother, and thus the prescribed nicknames. And Little Flad was lean and muscular like a split end, while Big Flad was huge as a defensive lineman, both being star athletes in high school, but having moved on to become hippies like everyone else.

And there were guys and gals whom Peter didn't know, adding to the gang, all huddled tightly, passing joints and drinking beer and snorting coke, trying to get as drunk and as high as drunkenness and its accompanying ascendency can go—and Jackson blended right in.

Roach's house had a musty smell, like lingering flatulence. The rosy evening sun filtered through a window milky with smoke resin. Fleas jumped off a dog of indeterminate breed on the carpet chewing on his own ass.

How different their lives had become, Peter pondered, since he himself had mellowed, softened, and self-righteously moved on from this decadence. He had erroneously assumed the others would have seen the light by now. It was only common sense to realize that drugs weren't the panacea originally ordained. Peter knew as much as anyone that nihilistic debauchery had had its ascetic and poetic moment, but it was only a moment—and then it was time to evolve. Such poetic license soon becomes disillusionment. But he saw that his old friends were not so inclined to move on. Lots of speed and downers now were gulped simultaneously in some sort of ironic indulgence that confused matters. Mostly, though, he could see it was the booze. It was the booze that carried this philosophical banter onwards in a more prolonged escape from reality. Drugs had opened their minds, sure; alcohol closed them back up. They preferred not being enlightened. They were all well into their twenties now and had moved on from this childish search for nirvana. They were living lives Peter had once admired as anti-establishment rebellion but had now just become laziness, intoxication, and decadence.

"Peter!" they all exclaimed melodramatically, as if some lost hero had finally come home, asking what the fuck he was up to these days, man—*working? Going to school? No shit! How 'bout fucking that, man!*

"Got my twenty bucks, Jacky?" Big Flad said to Jackson, who was busy rolling another joint.

Jackson said, "Actually I don't, Marv. But I get my first paycheck Friday, I'll pay ya then fer sure."

Big Flad nodded acquiescently, well aware that it was simply a matter of catching Jackson some time when he had twenty bucks on him, and he would pay it back, with interested compounded daily.

Jackson sealed a joint tight with an experienced flick of his tongue, took a rapacious toke, and handed it to Peter, who passed it on to Little Flad without taking a toke.

"Don't smoke dope anymore?" Little Flad said suspiciously, and Peter shook his head self-consciously.

"Why not," he said, like an accusation.

There had been a time when this altering of consciousness had been so incredibly vast and deep. Marijuana was a harmless weed that did not destroy brain cells; it only broadened awareness. It magnified existence. It made one aware of the exciting adventure of life. He had been able to see through people and into their soul. There were no bad people, only different people with different responses to their own particular environment. And the war, that fucking war; he was only now beginning to absorb the horror of it as if coming slowly out of a mind fuck. He now saw the uselessness of war, all wars. The Love Generation had adopted a new lifestyle and consciousness. They had shed the false formalities and silly etiquettes of a pretentious and commercial society. They were setting the fashion of a new age, only it wasn't fashionable, only ubiquitous. They were giving up their lease on society's established mores, on their stressful demands, on their nine-to-five farce—at last appreciating life. Status no longer mattered: All people were cool, man. This was a phenomenal new dawn; a change occurring that was more drastic and influential than any since the dawn of time. There was a new and different mood for love and a fierce demand for change. Their generation would set the standard for a new beginning free of oppression, repression, war, stress, racism. There would be a nurturing of the earth rather than raping it for profit.

The Love Generation would save the world.

If marijuana had given him an incredible new insight on life, then LSD had transcended that to a unique consciousness where the experience itself was concrete and physical, but the spoofing of the mind was a grotesque spoof on Being. The bodily sensations were subtly orgasmic; but the ventures of the mind were inexplicable, something so out of touch with normal existence as to be out of this world into another dimension of reality. It was terrifying to be so aware. He didn't know whether to accept this as a gathering of insight or to interpret it as a deranged twisting of consciousness. His mind moved too rapidly to comprehend any apparent message. It was an experience understood only by those who experienced it. People could assume what psychedelic meant, but they could never wholly understand it without experiencing it first hand.

It had decidedly altered his perception of life. He was being influenced, but it hadn't made sense; the experience altered reality as if he were seeing life through the kaleidoscope of schizophrenia, a schizophrenic who perhaps saw life as if really was, while everybody else were the crazy ones.

At any rate, Peter didn't know what to say to Flad. How does one explain that which no one can understand? All the initial effects from dope smoking that he had loved so much had suddenly reversed themselves. It was difficult understanding this himself much less articulating it. But he could no longer rationalize his continued indulgence to himself, much as he tried. While initially he had appreciated the insights it had given him, he later didn't enjoy it because it made him aware of the inequities and miseries of life rather than the beauty and happiness of it. While initially it had made him optimistic, it later made him intolerant. While initially it had relaxed him, later it made him anxious. While initially it had made him love and enjoy people, later it made him paranoid and suspicious of them. He was unable to respond to certain social situations in a rational, personable, articulate manner; he became panicky and withdrawn and could not arrange his thoughts into coherent conversation. He would blank out. He became depressed. It increased the poignancy of his personal problems, of the world situation, of pollution, and what seemed evident for posterity; and things didn't look good, man. When he was stoned he felt heavy and oppressed and over-loaded with the burden of living. It gave him a perspective of life he didn't want to behold. He didn't know whether marijuana distorted his grasp of reality or mirrored a true identity. It was representative of a time no longer there, done with. He had a family and responsibilities. When he quit smoking dope, he had accepted a sad passage of time. *The sixties are over, man.*

"I don't like it anymore," he told Flad.

"Tha's a good reason," Little Flad said, and smiled good-naturedly.

They sat and joints were smoked, and Peter almost felt as if he was getting a contact high. Then a couple emerged from underneath a blanket on the couch. Peter didn't recognize the dude, but the woman was Josephine. She had a weary, stoned look to her blurry/red eyes. She didn't say hello to Peter or Jackson, acting as if she didn't know either of them, as if she were a complete stranger. It was as if it wasn't Josephine, but some other person who looked like her. It was weird; tied into this surreal state of being these days somehow. *People are strange.*

"Let's get going," Jackson stood straight up, swallowing his beer.

But first he disappeared with Roach for a minute, returning from a transaction completed, resulting in a pronounced transformation.

———

It was seven p.m. They were hitchhiking again and in a few minutes got picked up by some high school kids. There were three boys and two girls, and now Peter and Jackson were in the front seat with the driver, and two boys were squeezed in with two girls in back, a girl sitting on a boy's lap. They were kissing and laughing. Everybody but Peter was smoking pot. Smoked drifted out the open windows in a white cloud like a scene from a Cheech and Chong movie.

Jackson told the driver where they were going, and the driver said he would take them as far as he could before he had to turn off. Jackson replied with his usual small talk about the car, about school, about drugs, and suddenly all of them seemed to be talking all at once, as if there was a need to impress Peter and Jackson with their precocious sophistication, all dying to place words in edgewise. One girl kept quiet though, Peter noticed. She seemed shy, her long dark hair covering most of her introverted face. Every time Peter turned to her she would smile shyly at him, even though Peter hadn't said one word, as though she suspected they were two of a kind, secluded and secure in their own private place, in a different time.

"Do the cops harass the kids much these days?" Jackson said.

"Not much," the driver said, shrugging. "The cops aren't too bad. A lot of them are friendly. One of them sells dope to the kids."

They drove a few blocks, then the driver said: "We want to turn here, but I s'ppose we can give you a ride further if you're in a hurry."

"I sorta am in fact," Jackson said. "No—wait! Never mind, I see somebody we know over there. We'll get out here."

Jackson was referring to an old white milk delivery van that was pulled over on the side of the road with some men leaning against it smoking and drinking beer. Peter recognized them—more former high school buddies whom he hadn't seen in years—probably since high school in fact.

They got out and thanked the kids for the ride, and the girl who had been flirting with Peter gave him one last desperate smile, making him think of all the great looking chicks there were in the world and here he was married.

They jogged over to the milk van and said their hellos, and since it was about eight years since Peter had seen any of them, it was strange how they greeted him, as if it had been just the other day. And they all carried the tell-tale marks of drinking and drugging these last years, especially Guy Mitchell, the apparent owner of the old retired milk van, who had been big time in high school (football star, basketball star, straight-A student, voted most likely to succeed) but who was now overweight and overwrought and at this particular moment particularly drunk.

What's happening to this Love Generation? pondered Peter not for the first time. And what caused it? Drugs? Nixon's Counterinpro? Vietnam? Doctor Spock? Timothy Leary? Abbie Hoffman? Jane Fonda? Stanley Owsley? At any rate, Guy Mitchell, most likely to succeed from the class of '66, stood before Peter like a tall old drunk. Peter was amazed. But Jackson talked to him like a close friend whom he talked to every day of the week.

"We need a ride, Guy."

"Where to?"

"I need a ride to work, and Peter needs a ride home."

Guy shrugged. "No gas, man."

Jackson dug deeply into his faded old Levi's and emerged with a rumpled dollar bill.

Guy chuckled sarcastically at the paltry significance one dollar would make to his gas-guzzling panel truck in this era of climbing gas prices. *Fuck, it just went over a dollar a gallon last week; whoda ever thought? Next thing ya know we'll be paying a buck for a pack a smokes.* But he snatched the buck away from Jackson anyway. "Get in," he said with a tone of frustration.

He gave them a frightening, drunken ride, first Jackson to work, then Peter to home, and he thanked Guy ever so much for the ride, and thanked God for getting him home in one piece.

He was hungry and horny, and Caitlin was serving dinner. She gave him a dirty look.

ELEVEN

Peter completed his master's degree and was working on his teacher's certificate. Caitlin became pregnant again and suddenly he was the father of two boys, Thomas and Fitzgerald, two boys he would come to love like a song, a beautiful song. He loved his family, and couldn't imagine never having them. He was a family man.

Despite that, at the sheet metal shop he found himself attracted to a welder, the only woman welder in the shop. She got attention. Not beautiful, but magnetic and prismatic; alarmingly striking and out there. She was tall, about five-foot-nine, only unusual because she was half Chinese. Her name was Glenda Woo. Her sensuously lazy eyes were prism black. Wide, thin lips and high protruding cheekbones surrounded a delicate nose. Her smooth white skin was flawless except for a nose ring. She never wore a bra under the blue denim work shirts she perpetually wore, and her well endowed bosom slowed production as she bobbed and weaved and wiggled her tightly jeaned ass down the aisle in her audacious and pragmatic gait.

They talked, and she confessed to Peter her leftist leanings, and wondered how he would react, since most of the workers there were boneheaded Republicans. Peter confided in her these same leanings. Despite this harmonious propensity, they discovered profound differences in opinion about "The Revolution". She believed in the inevitability of armed revolution while Peter had faith in the democratic process, adopting a socialist system methodically and systematically.

"It should be obvious to you by now, Peter, dear, that the establishment will never let that happen. They own the legislatures. They own the media. The government is fascist, and they will never let democracy get in the way of their agenda. They will sabotage it by whatever means they deem necessary. The masses are so influenced and manipulated by the ruling class that they are shifting more to the *right* than the left. Look who we have for president for crissakes: Nixon!"

"They are now, but as more and more people do with less while the ruling class gets richer and richer, the people will become aware of the evils behind private predatory capitalism and throw it out. We're certainly not going to recruit support by blowing up buildings or shooting at people, the way the George Jackson Brigade is going about it. That only alienates everyone."

"The Brigade goes out of its way to avoid shooting people, Peter. They're *too* cautious, if you ask me. We can't sit around fatalistically on our asses expecting things to happen. We have to act! The elitists have too much power and will continue to initiate this power through a bourgeois media. The only solution is to overwhelm this propaganda and oppression through armed revolution!"

"'Revolutions have never lifted the burden of tyranny, only shifted the onus of oppression onto another's shoulder'. George Bernard Shaw."

"*Fuck* Shaw, that impotent old fuck! You pacifists make me puke!"

He *was* a pacifist. Vietnam made sure of that. He believed in socialism, but his political commitments were not so well defined as diehard Marxists. He had read Marx of course, and wasn't so sure of its complete dogma. He had a major issue with the confiscation of private property. Everyone deserves a place of one's own. He was all too aware of how different individual philosophy was as to arrive at any definitive consensus. It hadn't happened yet in the history of civilization.

Peter laughed. "It's lunchtime. Let's go."

Peter and Glenda ran three miles every day at lunchtime. They had half an hour; just enough time to strip down, run three miles at a pretty good clip, return to work, stretch for a couple minutes, then dress—all the time talking nonstop.

One Saturday they ran around Green Lake then went to her apartment where she fixed him breakfast like any proper subordinate woman would then grabbed his hand and led him to bed. He was shocked at how tight she was; she held his penis and wouldn't allow total penetration, grunting as if he was hurting her.

"I have a confession," Glenda said, afterwards.

"You've never fucked a married man before."

"Oh, Peter, you are so funny, hardyharhar!"

"You're married and have five children."

"You are so cold, so way off, way *way* off!"

"Okay, I give."

"The fact is, Peter love, I belong to a sexual minority."

"You're bi."

"Yes, of course I am, love, isn't everyone? But no, I belong to another sexual minority, one much more in the minority as homosexuality."

There was a suspenseful pause. She licked her ruby lips and blinked her chocolate eyes, smiling facetiously as always. "Since we have now become intimate, I will tell you the T and nothing but the T about myself and that is, love, that I am a transsexual."

"Uh huh," Peter said, not believing her of course.

But she remained silent a moment, allowing densely brained Peter to slowly grasp this reality.

"No," he said.

She nodded firmly, laughing. "That is the absolute T about me."

He stared methodically. "No."

She shrugged stolidly.

"But...you had an orgasm!" Peter stammered. "...Didn't you?"

"I have orgasms like men have orgasms. They leave glands in the operation that react to stimulus just like you do and result in orgasms just like you."

"I can't believe this."

"You can't believe it, or you don't want to believe it?"

"But you're so...You look so...You're not anything at all like a..."

"Man? But Peter, dear, that's the whole point."

"But I mean, I never would have suspected in a million years."

"Yes, I know. No one has ever guessed."

"Are you sure?"

"Oh, Peter, dear, you are so funny! Hardyharhar!"

Peter drove home in a state of disbelief and shame. It was the first time he had been unfaithful to Caitlin since they had married, and with a transsexual! "Oh my God," he said out loud.

TWELVE

Peter, Perry, Paul, and Jackson planned a bicycle trip over to the Olympic Mountains. They rode to the Fauntleroy ferry dock and took the ferry to Southworth, then meandered the undulating back roads to Kingston—where they decided to spend the night.

Resting on the lawn at a public park beside their bikes, they watched a softball game in progress. After the game was over, there was a series of other fun athletic events being organized, one of which was the 100 yard dash. The Placik brothers looked at each other and laughed. They rushed over to participate. Altogether, there were about forty men lined up. The gun went off. About ten or eleven seconds later Peter had won.

Back at the bikes Paul was complaining that Perry had grabbed onto his shirt and held him back. "Otherwise I would have won." Peter looked at Perry for confirmation, but he was laughing.

"I still would have won," Peter said.

"Bullshit," Paul said. Paul was sixteen and carried the arrogance of adolescence, an arrogance that would accompany him into adulthood.

"Okay," Peter said, "Let's go it again."

The three brothers walked over to the starting line. Perry said go. When Peter finished, again in about ten or eleven seconds, he turned around to look and saw both the brothers standing on the starting line pointing at him and laughing.

Just then a Volkswagen camper pulled up into the parking lot and a bunch of long-haired hippies piled out. Peter recognized Roach right away and then six-foot-four Stan Coblen, whom everyone called "Stork" emerged, and Josephine, Josephine's sister Lynn, and a friend of the sisters, whom everyone called "Matty." Matty had massive breasts she managed to haul around behind a thin white tank top, and thread bare denim jeans cut off practically at her crotch.

All of a sudden everyone was smoking dope and drinking beer. Seeing that their bicycle excursion had now been turned into a full blown party, and knowing full well that Jackson had been the instigator behind this, Peter snatched a beer and fumed. He was not happy. But a few beers later around the camp fire he shrugged and reluctantly joined in. Matty dropped her huge ass down next to him and said: "You and your brothers are somethin' else—the best looking guys around."

Peter didn't respond to what was obvious and jumped up and stormed off, fuming, she following with a middle finger running up the rear seam of his jeans. Striking out here, she tried her luck with Perry, but he had already hooked up with Lynn. Desperate, she stumbled with her beer over to sixteen-year-old Paul, who was nonplussed by this old woman's attentions. She carried on resolutely, from guy to guy, none of whom seemed much interested.

Suddenly, Matty and Jackson got into the VW camper and drove off, Josephine watching them go. "Where the fuck they goin'?" she said.

No one knew.

When they returned an hour later she said: "Where the fuck you two go off to?"

"To get more beer," Jackson said, carrying two cases of Bud as alibi.

"Uh huh," Josephine said.

Matty ignored her prying eyes.

That night, while everyone was trying to sleep, Lynn kept everyone awake with her ecstatic squeals. They went on all night. In the morning, Perry and Lynn squirmed their way out of their tent looking bright eyed and bushy-tailed.

THIRTEEN

As a result of that trip and others, Jackson fell in love with the Olympic peninsula and got a job at Pulp and Talbot in Poulsbo, and bought a small log cabin with a wood burning stove. He had acquired the home in the country he had been talking about for years, and moved Josephine in with him. They had a dog and two goats to keep the weeds down. It was mid-summer, and they had a vegetable garden of tomatoes, corn, squash, and a small healthy plot of marijuana.

One Friday night Peter picked Josephine up at the Fauntleroy ferry to take her to fill a prescription for pain medication for Jackson. Apparently Jackson had hurt his back at work at the lumber mill. Jackson would spend the rest of his life collecting disability insurance because of this back injury and never work again at a regular job. The feds would frequently attempt to take this benefit away from him, but he would obtain the services of a lawyer and eventually be granted a full disability receiving 80% of the prevailing wages at the lumber mill for the rest of his life. But we're getting ahead of ourselves again.

Peter and Josephine were on the Fauntleroy ferry back to Southworth. He was going to spend the weekend with them. Peter had brought a fifth of Seagram's with him, and after they had each drunk a pint of beer at the cafeteria, Josephine said: "7-Up!" "What?" Peter said. "7-Up!" and ran off excitedly and returned with two large cups, one empty and one full of 7-Up. She emptied half the contents of the 7-Up into the empty cup then helped herself to the Seagram's, cracking the seal and topping off both cups.

By the time they reached Southworth, they were having a grand old time. Josephine couldn't keep her hands off him, and Peter kept pushing her away, laughing hysterically. Josephine laughed back and wouldn't stop groping him.

By the time they arrived at Indianola, Jackson did not look happy to see them.

"What took you so long!" he rather exclaimed. "I was in so much pain I had to open this!" He held up a half empty fifth of peach brandy.

"What the fuck!" Josephine snapped back. "I told the ferry captain to step on it, but he refused to obey!"

"Did you get my pain pills?" Jackson said.

"Yes, I got your fucking pain pills."

Jackson limped over with a pain-filled grimace and took the pills. "It's been opened!" he exclaimed with dismay.

"I had a headache," she explained.

He tossed two into his mouth and swallowed them with a slug of peach brandy.

Josephine fixed herself another whiskey/seven and took two more pain pills. "Do you have a headache too per chance, Peter?"

Peter laughed and said no. "And it says right there on the prescription bottle you're not supposed to mix that with alcohol."

Jackson and Josephine looked at each other. "Okay, mom!" they both chimed harmoniously, and laughed.

This annoyed Peter, realizing that he was being made fun of—again. He went in to fix himself another drink, only to find the bottle he had brought to last the entire weekend practically empty.

Jackson immediately started making sarcastic comments about how the pills were dong a commendable job of fucking up his head but doing absolutely *nada* fucking thing to alleviate the horrific pain in his back that ran all the way down out the end of his toes. "And the greedy fuckers expect me to go back to work like this!"

He had been in the hospital two weeks previous for treatment on his back. They had him in traction, and he wouldn't stop complaining about his back until they finally gave in and hooked up to an IV feeding him morphine. During this long and torturous week, he was now explaining to Peter loudly and angrily, they performed something like a spinal tap. "I asked the anesthesiologist if it was a spinal tap, and he said it was and it wasn't—whatever the fuck that means! The surgeon then said, for what reason I immediately became suspicious, that there had only been five cases in medical history of anything going wrong with this particular procedure—and it is now obvious that I am the sixth, since I have had this horrific headache, and the fucking pain meds aren't doing squat on the pot for that either! I'm going to throw a malpractice suit on the hospital, the doctor, and the anesthesiologist and sue the lumber mill to boot!" He in fact demanded that Josephine get her fat ass on the phone right this minute and call him a fucking lawyer before he dropped dead from an aneurism and they were left with nothing!

Josephine picked up the phone receiver and said into it: "You're a fucking lawyer," then slammed it back down.

Peter and Josephine laughed hysterically. She started groping Peter again.

"Very funny. Very, very funny. Here I am about to drop dead from a stroke and you're making fun—instead of dinner. Yeah, what about soma that? You hungry, Peter?"

"I could eat."

"Hear that, Josephine? Our guest says he's hungry."

"Your legs broken?" Josephine said.

"No, but my fucking back is, goddammit!"

She jumped up and ran out of the room. Peter thought she was making fun again, going in immediately to start preparing dinner in sarcastic reaction to his demand. But instead she ran to the bathroom. They could hear the vomiting of the fifth Peter had brought for the weekend.

Jackson hurried into the bathroom to check on her, and then gently escorted her to bed. Then out he went to the kitchen to toss a couple burgers on the grill, returning to Peter in the living room hauling a couple of beers.

Suddenly he was maudlin. There were tears in his eyes as he related to Peter the perfect relationship he and Josephine had, how loyal and faithful they were to each other—the first girlfriend he had ever been faithful to, how they never *ever* fought.

Then Josephine reappeared suddenly, stumbling across the bare hard-wood floor barefoot, and it seemed they embarked on their very first ever fight. What they were arguing about Peter wasn't sure, but he thought it had something to do with the dinner she had been expected to fix.

"This is the seventies, goddammit! Or haven't ya heard? Men're s'possed to help out 'round the house nowadays!"

"Wait a minute!" Jackson protested. "I don't see you getting your ass up everyday and going to work!"

"I don't see you doin' it neither!"

"Only because of my back! You expect me to slave over that fucking stove the way my back is?"

"Oh, get off that shit. There's nothing wrong with your back. You and Peter are always playing tennis and going out in the woods cutting firewood! Who does that shit with a bad back?"

"It comes and goes," he explained. "Hey, Peter, speaking of cutting fire-wood, did ya hear 'bout the Pollack who went to the hardware store and asked for the best chain saw they got. The storekeeper handed him one and said, 'You'll cut five cords of wood a day with *this* chainsaw!' So the Pollack went out in the woods and worked his *ass* off all day and only got his pickup half full. All pissed off, he took the chain saw back to the hardware store and complained. The storekeeper said, 'Huh, let's see', grabbed the chain saw, pulled the string, and started it up. The Pollack jumped back 'bout six feet and said, 'What's that noise!'"

Jackson and Josephine roared with laughter.

Peter said, "Hey, Jackson, whaddaya get when you mix one mick with another mick?"

"What?"

"A drunken idiot."

Josephine laughed.

"That s'pposed to be funny?"

Suddenly, for no reason that Peter could detect, Jackson and Josephine proceeded to exchange vicious obscenities back and forth.

"Peter!" Jackson now turned to him, grabbing onto his back with another pain-racked grimace. "When you return to Seattle take this fucking bitch with you!"

"Oh, fuck off," she said calmly and returned to the bedroom.

Jackson chased after her. Peter went into the kitchen to check on the burg-ers all the while listening to the crashing and banging emanating from the bed-room—then just a rhythmic banging that lasted about a minute, after which

Jackson emerged from the bedroom straight backed and smug, a satisfied grin on his face. "I guess I showed her," he said. "Let's eat."

———

Jackson had gained about twenty pounds on his once lithe, muscular frame. He had the first indication of a middle-aged spread, though he was not yet thirty. Saturday morning after coffee and scrambled eggs, they drove over to the local tennis court and played a set of tennis, Peter winning 6-0, then Jackson said he was done: "My back."

They returned to the house for a beer.

Billy, a friend of Jackson's, was there. He was nineteen and barely had to shave, his whiskers sparse and white. Peter liked Billy instantly. He was a nice guy, the kind of guy Jackson unconsciously exploited. Billie asked Jackson if Jackson had any of the money he owed him, and Jackson said: "I don't, Billy, those fuckers keep delaying my disability checks, but I'll have it for you next week by hook or fuckin' crook, man, I really will."

"I...I...It's...co...cool," Billy stammered.

When he left Peter asked Jackson if Billy's last name was Bibbitt.

"No. Why?"

"You know, *One Flew Over the Cuckoo's Nest.*"

"Oh," Jackson said, understanding the joke but not laughing. It was ironic that Jackson used people, but never made fun of them. It occurred to Peter that Jackson never said anything bad about anyone.

Peter and Jackson walked over to a farm house close by where Jackson and Josephine got their fresh raw milk and farm fresh eggs. "That milk tastes like sweet ice cream, man, and the eggs are almost as big as my fist and sweet as candy. Ya put one egg into the pancake batter and it turns it Halloween orange it's so rich."

The farmer they bought their eggs and milk from had a hideous deformity in his head, an indentation that appeared like a three-inch shelf in the middle of his forehead. When they left, Peter asked Jackson about it. Apparently, about thirty years before, his head had collided with the back end of a flatbed truck and caused the indentation.

During the weekend Peter observed Jackson consume with seemingly little effect: two fifths of peach brandy, most of a bottle of Percocet, one fifth of whiskey, about twelve beers, about twenty joints, a gram of hash, and a gram of cocaine. Peter was impressed; he could never do that.

Later that day Caitlin arrived in the Honda Civic with the two boys, who excitedly ran up to Peter and into his arms. Caitlin was immediately disgusted with her brother's inebriated condition, as if expecting him to be different from any other time.

That night they all went into town for dinner and a movie, *Carnal Knowledge*, with Jack Nicholson, Art Garfunkel, Ann Margaret, and Candice Bergin. Peter gasped and his eyes popped out of his head when it came to Ann Margaret's nude scene, complete front and back. Jackson and Josephine slept throughout the film.

———

At home later Caitlin came out of the bedroom and said that while she was sitting on the pot her IUD plopped into the toilet with the pee. She had had nothing but trouble with this contraceptive device ever since it had been inserted. She had gained weight and experienced constant nausea and headaches. She had gone to the doctor about it, but the doctor said they were unrelated. But right after purging the IUD, her headaches and nausea went away and never came back and her weight stabilized. The IUD was called the Dalkon Shield. Years later they would receive a letter from the government asking if they wanted to be part of a class action suit against the Dalkon Corporation and the A.H. Robins Company, or else settle out of court for $700. They would need the cash. They would settle.

Peter decided to get a vasectomy, which was a relief for Caitlin and for Peter in more ways than one. But Caitlin's relief would soon turn to anguish.

FOURTEEN

Peter got his teaching certificate and a position at Seattle Community College teaching American Literature. He had to quit his job at Alaskan Copper Works, which meant a reduction in pay and belt tightening at home.

He was thirty. He panicked about this, as if his youth had been unfairly yanked out from under him without warning. He had an affair with one of his students.

Her name was Liana. Her father was living and working for some oil billionaire in Iran and sent home oodles of money for Liana and her mother. Liana paid for everything when they went out. This was nice, but Peter worried about her post-adolescence, little- rich-girl temper tantrums. She couldn't care less about Melville, Faulkner, Hemingway, or Fitzgerald and was more interested in drugs, punk rock, animation, and David Bowie. She was flunking out, but he felt obligated to pass her—then broke it off.

And anyway, he was becoming more interested in a colleague, a very serious English Lit teacher who was six years older than he. Her name was Myra. She played tennis and climbed mountains, she told him, and the tennis offered him the opportunity for that which he had been conspiring toward. She was upset when he beat her 6-4, 6-2. Myra seemed to lack a certain sense of humor, he realized; self-confident, poised, and always prepared for a life full of conflicts. She had begun to show grey in her short straight hair and didn't bother to color it.

"Do you climb?" she said, challengingly, right after the tennis.

"No."

"A Northwesterner all your life and never climbed?"

"I didn't say never. I've done Rainier and done a lot of hiking in the Olympics and Cascades."

"Mount Rainier is a hike," she said, downplaying an accomplishment of which he had been personally proud, as proud as he had been when he ran the Seattle Marathon.

"I like to hike, but frankly, I'm not into the more extreme sports. I admit it: I'm a coward. I will never climb Everest or hang glide or parachute."

"Parachuting and hang gliding is fun not scary," she argued.

His calculated seduction had seemed to have run into a slight barrier.

"I suppose you've bungee jumped too."

"Sure."

"I've climbed Mount Si five times." He shrugged, not knowing what else to say.

This finally elicited a laugh.

"How about this weekend then?" she said.

"Mount Si?"

"Sure."

"You got a date."

Mount Si was a fairly strenuous hike, but not so strenuous that sixty-year-old grandmothers didn't do it every weekend. And Peter was impressed with Myra's conditioning as they switch-backed past other hikers in their ascension. He thought they were clipping along pretty well, until a runner wearing nothing but shorts and shoes scooted past them like they were standing still.

They arrived at the top, except for "The haystack", which was a hand-over-hand climb of some difficulty. Myra immediately started scrambling up, and Peter had no choice but to follow. It wasn't that bad, it turned out, and offered a sweeping view of the Cascades and in the smoggy distance the caps of Seattle skyscrapers.

They sat and nibbled carrot sticks, cheese, and apple slices, then Myra stood and scampered back down without a word.

Heading back down I-90 towards Issaquah, he asked if she wanted to stop for a drink.

"I have booze at my place," she said.

At her house in Bellevue, she handed him a rum and coke, and said: "We haven't much time. My ex will be here soon with the kids," and it was off to the bedroom for a quickie before the ex-hubbie indeed arrived on time with the young son and daughter before Peter barely had time to finish his drink.

"So you're Myra's new boyfriend," the ex said to Peter, shaking his hand.

"Um…" Peter said.

"He's not my boyfriend, Cal. We're colleagues and hiking buddies is all."

"Ah," he said, but winked at Peter as if they held a guy secret.

He looked about forty, as tall as Peter, but heavier, pudgy with thinning hair.

The ex left, the children went out to play, and Peter and Myra had another drink.

"I'll be frank with you, Peter, I'm not interested in a romance here, just some good times."

"Well…I am married after all."

"Yes, of course. That is convenient, isn't it? I was married for some time, and I know the game."

The game?

"How about a hike next weekend?" she said.

"Sounds good."

"How about we make it a weekend thing, with a tent and everything."

"I'll have to work it out. I'll let you know."

"Of course you will."

———

Monday at school Peter told Myra it was a go for the weekend.

Saturday morning they drove to Central Washington to hike into Lake Ingalls. It was a three-miler, but no switchbacks like Mount Si, practically straight up over jutting boulders and sharp grey terrain, involving some "scrambling," as Myra called it. It was a popular spot for rock climbers, she had said, and most of the people they would encounter would be there to challenge the precarious rocks that surrounded the lake.

It was late September, and one possibility the seasoned climber Myra had neglected to account for was suddenly changing weather. It had been sunny and warm when they left Seattle, but they were met by a sudden stiff wind from the north as they stepped out of their vehicle into the parking lot, and they had not thought to bring winter clothes.

The farther they hiked the windier and colder it got, though they kept warm with the exertion of the climb.

While they were resting for a bit, a group of rock climbers approached. They had British accents, and one of them, a cute blonde who was vaguely familiar, kept staring at Peter curiously.

"Didn't I see you in Switzerland this year?" she said to him.

"No, I skipped the Alps this year."

But to add to the *déjà vu* eeriness of the encounter, he was sure he had seen her too somewhere before.

"Ever been to England?" she said.

"No."

"Australia?"

"No. What's your name?"

"Sandy Clinch."

Peter nodded, and kept staring at her, convinced that he had seen her somewhere before.

Myra seemed annoyed at the attention these two were paying each other, and said: "Peter…Shall we go?"

They reached the lake. Peter looked around. It looked portentous and eerie, a perfect locale for a science fiction movie, he thought. The environment was still and lifeless, not the peep of a bird, not the jump of a fish in the lake. Sharp rocks jutted hundreds of feet into the air, populated with rock climbers.

Dark foreboding clouds ambled in and hovered. Peter shivered.

"Let's pitch the tent," Myra said.

They put up the tent and built a fire and ate lunch, watching the rock climbers pulling themselves athletically up the rocks. He spotted Sandy. He waved at her, but though she seemed to have paused in her climb to look at him, she didn't wave back.

"We'll have to try it sometime," Myra said.

"What?"

"Rock climbing of course."

"I don't think so. It's just hiking and tennis for this cowboy."

"Oh, don't be such a wuss." She appeared serious.

She looked up at the grey sky which was growing increasingly dark and seemed to be thinking. "Rain," she said, and sure enough before they had finished their coffee it began to pour cats and dogs.

They tossed their gear inside the tent and scampered in. They were shivering. They zipped their goose down bags together, got naked, and crawled inside, rubbing each other warm, and soon were making love.

And afterwards they turned away from each other and dozed.

Then it stopped raining. They got dressed and crawled outside. The climbers were gone. The evening was growing dim. They got the fire going again and drank cognac before dinner, which Peter fixed while Myra gathered firewood.

After dinner they huddled by the fire and sipped cognac. It warmed their innards.

"You know," Myra lectured, "alcohol doesn't really keep you warm. The warmth you feel is actually heat leaving your body."

Peter knew this of course: He was a college graduate. "Whatever. I'm warm as toast right now."

The bottle emptied, Myra turned sentimental, talking about her ex-husband in a loving way, how he had been a good husband and father, but he had started to bore her. She'd had affairs, she admitted. Then she started to cry. Peter knew this was due more to the cognac than nostalgia and put his arms around her and drew her to him while she sobbed against his shoulder.

They returned to the tent and fucked their brains out.

———

In the morning Myra shook Peter awake. "Peter! Look outside!"

Peter put his head outside the part in the tent and was greeted with a glori-
ous sunrise. But in front of the sun was a terrain of pure, glistening white.

"It snowed." He fell back inside the tent and laughed.

"Yes, and we're in trouble."

"Why?"

"We can't hike back in that! I don't know if we can find the trail!"

"Oh."

"We're fucked."

"Oh well, as long as we're fucked—let's fuck!"

"Peter, this is serious."

They quickly dressed, rebuilt the fire with numb fingers, and fixed coffee.

"You don't think we should try hiking down?"

"You don't understand. The only thing to do is stay put and wait for a
rescue party."

"Oh. This *is* serious."

"I *told* you. It's why we left our names at the base, for emergency rescue."

They kept busy gathering firewood, keeping the blaze up to keep them
warm and to signal a rescue party. They munched sparingly on what food they
had, having brought only enough for dinner the night before and breakfast that
morning. They melted snow for drinking water and coffee.

They sat by the fire and read. Myra was reading May Sarton's *A Season of
Solitude.* Peter was reading Mikhail Petrovich Artzybashev's *Sanine.*

They went for a short hike. Everything seemed lifeless, frozen. They gathered more firewood. It became black and ice cold. Hope for a rescue party
dimmed with the fading light.

"Now I'm wondering if they're even looking for us," Myra said despairingly. "They have to know we're up here. I don't understand."

There was nothing for them to do but turn in. They were no longer in the
mood for love. Their little hiking venture had now become a tense drama.

So they passed another night, and it was Monday morning. They crawled
outside and gasped. They looked around in disbelief. It had snowed about a
foot more during the night, and it was *still* snowing. They peered up into the
sky and saw nothing but white.

"They'll never find us through this," she said.

Peter stared at her in a panic. "They won't?"

"Peter." She stared at Peter like at a child with whom one has lost patience.

With cold, biting hands, they gathered more firewood in gloomy silence. The situation now appeared desperate. They piled kindling onto the last of their newspaper and relit the fire.

"We're probably a sensation at school now," Myra said.

"Yeah?"

"It's probably all over the local news that a couple hikers are missing."

"Did you tell anyone you were going?"

"When I left the kids at my ex-husband's I told him where I was going and with whom."

They sat thinking by the fire. At 11:30 a.m. the snow had let up some. But there was now about two feet of snow on the ground.

"If it doesn't stop snowing by early afternoon we might as well go," she said.

"Hike down?"

"We'll probably fall somewhere and kill ourselves, but I don't know what else to do. The snow may not melt now until spring. We'll just have to calibrate each step very carefully. For whatever reason, it doesn't appear a rescue party is coming. We're out of food. We're freezing. We don't have any paper to start a fire. We don't have the proper clothing. We'll freeze to death if we stay."

They were hungry and shivering from the cold. They couldn't wrap themselves with the down sleeping bag because it would get wet. They couldn't go inside the tent because they needed to be out there in case a helicopter came. They kept piling dead branches on the fire.

At one p.m. it had stopped snowing. But the snow was replaced with an icy fog.

"Fuck it," Myra said, jumping up. "Let's get the hell out of here."

They quickly packed. Myra looked at her compass and said: "Ready?"

They began their descent. They put wool socks on their hands and began feeling their way down. They weren't even sure they were on the trail. They were about fifty yards away from camp when Myra called out: "Listen!"

Peter listened, but heard nothing. "What is it?"

"Shhh!"

There was a faint buzzing sound, like the sound of a refrigerator fan.

It grew louder.

"It's a helicopter!" she cried.

An immense figure materialized out of the frozen white, hovering above like a monstrous insect. A man peered out of the passenger side and waved.

"I didn't think you guys were coming," Myra said to the man who was lowered down to help them get loaded in the lift.

"We didn't start looking until late yesterday. The ranger's been sick and nobody checked the list until late in the day when it was too dark."

"We were starting to hike down," Peter said.

"It's lucky we got here when we did then. You never would have made it."

Myra looked at Peter and shrugged. Peter sighed with relief and smiled.

FIFTEEN

And of course Caitlin suspected that Peter hadn't gone on a weekend hike with a "friend" all along, as he had said, and now her suspicion was confirmed.

"I can't take it anymore," she said.

"All right."

"I'm serious, Peter. I thought I could learn to live with it until you got it out of your system, but I can't. If you can't stay away from other women, you will have to leave."

"All right."

"It's that easy for you."

"I don't want to lose you and the boys. You are too important to me. I love you."

She glared at him in amazement. "You could at least *act* like you mean it."

"I do mean it. Where are the boys?"

"Now you wonder where the boys are. They've been at mom and dad's since yesterday."

"I love you and the boys. You know that."

"I know you do, Peter. I know you. But I'm not sure the boys know. You might try paying them more attention. And if you don't break if off with that woman, it's over."

So he did; he broke it off with Myra.

And almost immediately found himself infatuated with another of his students.

Billie wore thick, horn-rimmed glasses which gave her an intellectual look, had small breasts and a large round derriere.

"Why did you choose me?" she said, after they had made love at her apartment on Capitol Hill close to campus.

"Did I choose you? I thought we chose each other."

"But there are loads of students prettier than I. You could have any one of them."

"That's not true at all, and anyway, I was interested in you."

"Why?"

"I find you attractive."

"But I'm not. I'm not attractive at all."

"Yes, you are…but anyway…It's more than your physical body…I was attracted to your essay about Henry James."

"But what if we fall in love?"

"You're not in love with me now?"

She laughed. "You're the one who's supposed to be logical here, the experienced older mentor. I'm just a flawed, naïve little girl."

"Little flawed naïve Liberty McDowell."

She laughed. "Maybe not that flawed, at least physically, or naïve."

"We won't fall in love then."

"I didn't know love was a choice!"

She rolled a joint and lit it. She held it out to him while holding it in. He shook his head. "No thanks."

"Don't smoke?"

"I have a class to teach this afternoon." He was in no mood to explain.

"And I have a class to attend. So what?"

They laughed.

So they wouldn't fall I love. So what was this vague visceral feeling that was developing? It *seemed* sort of like falling in love. He found himself thinking about her day and night. It hadn't even occurred to him whether or not she was pretty; he didn't care. Her face was fixed clearly in his mind yet curiously had no perspective, no distinct prejudice. She became an idea, not an object. This was dangerous, he knew; he was jumping without a chute. Though the relationship was new, he had this idea of it lasting a long time. She would be his mistress, he decided. The problem was, he hadn't the money to properly provide for a mistress. Would she understand? Nevertheless, he saw himself subservient to her, subject to her every wish, tied around her finger, as they say, a state since Eva he had decided never again to inhabit. Bitch or Goddess, queen or sorceress; he was obsessed with this idea, insanely infatuated with a woman, barely a woman, almost an adolescent. She *was* an adolescent! She was nineteen, a teenager!

Sunday at noon he called her to confirm a date. She told him she had gone to a party with her roommate the night before and was hungover. "It was a great party," she said, almost as if rubbing it in. "They were all people my age—young people."

What's she saying? Was she implying that he was not young? "Anyhoo," he said, "today."

"Not today, I don't think."

"Oh! All right!"

"See you tomorrow in class."

He was always assuming women would fall head over heels in love with him regardless. When he was in this hyper state, every woman in the world was checking him out, when not, he was suddenly invisible. Though he knew instinctively all the Placik men were good looking, tall, dark, and brooding—more than good looking. Even the old man, his dissipated six-foot-four shrunk to nearly Peter's height now; pot-bellied, triple-chinned, and grey—even he was still a fine figure of manhood.

But when he became depressed he would wonder why any woman would have anything to do with him at all. It had been a long time since he had felt this way about a woman, and she seemed to be playing him for a high school kid. He didn't like playing games; never had. If he had learned anything from his experience with Eva it was to handle rejection with dignity and grace. If a woman liked him, fine; if not, so what, move on. It's why Maugham's *Of Human Bondage* irritated him to no end; he couldn't imagine tolerating a situation like that of Maugham's pitiful protagonist.

He decided he must end it before it had begun. To react in any other fashion was humiliating. It was simple.

Though not so simple as for him to not be driven nuts the following week as she completely ignored him in class. He was lecturing Hemingway's *The Old Man and the Sea*, a small book, a novella, practically a short story, simple yet complex with metaphoric life challenges, stark prose, the sea representing lost hope, success and failure, all facets of the same existence…blah blah blah…Nevertheless, along with *The Sun Also Rises*, Hemingway's finest novel, in his humble opinion.

But Billie looked bored. She hated Hemingway; she said he was an over-rated, alcoholic, chauvinist, anti-Semitic pig. True, perhaps, but Hemingway was an important figure in American literature and thus part of his god-damned, mother-fucking class, goddamn it! He was pissed. He had planned to assign an essay of 1,000-words, and changed it to 1,500-words. Billie sighed audibly.

After class he saw her approach him out of his peripheral vision. He ignored her.

"Wanna get some coffee?"

"Let's see, let me check my schedule." He pretended to pencil something into his desk calendar. "B-U-S…Sorry, I'm busy."

She laughed.

"Lessgo."

At the coffee house on Broadway Avenue she said: "I'm sorry about Sunday."

He nodded and said: "I don't like playing games."

"I'm not playing games, I'm confused."

"Then why not just say that? What are you confused about?"

"What do you think? You're a married man! I had decided it was not wise to get involved. After my last boyfriend I had decided to be chaste for a year."

"How long did that last?"

"About a month."

They laughed and he leaned forward to touch her chin tenderly. She regarded him soberly. "You're a charmer."

"You may be right," he said. "This may not work."

She nodded agreeably. But she looked miserable, which was encouraging. "And I don't know if I like you spending most of your time with your wife."

"But I'll be thinking of you. I've been thinking of nothing but."

"Really?" She looked surprised.

He shook his head. "You're driving me crazy."

Now she touched his chin in this same condescending manner. "What's wrong?"

"I shouldn't be telling you this."

She backed away, looking serious again. "You think? It's one reason why I did what I did Sunday."

"I don't like that. I don't like it when you say you'll see me, and then don't."

"Now you're acting possessive."

"Don't throw that shit at me. If I'm being possessive, so what. Anyway, I'm not. All you have to say is go away and I'll go away—just like that." He snapped his fingers. It startled her.

She grabbed onto his hands and clutched them. She tickled his palms, looking searchingly into his eyes.

"I can see the kind of relationship we would have," he said.

"Oh? And what's that?"

"We'd fight all the time but not be able to stop seeing each other because we'd be so much in love."

She smiled, seeming to like this idea. He certainly didn't. He had known relationships like that. Perry and Lynn were in a relationship like that. His common sense told him to end it now. But he liked this feeling of being in love. It was intoxicating, like a drug. He liked the drug and dreaded the withdrawal, which was inevitable.

It was Halloween. He had to rush home and take the boys trick or treating. He had promised Caitlin.

"Come buy candy with me!" Billie demanded.

"I really have to go. It's getting dark."

She frowned.

Peter had a pair of complimentary tickets to a Sonics game scheduled for the following Friday. He asked Billie to go, and was a little surprised to learn that she was a basketball fan. She was from Portland, and part of the Blazermania that had swept the city the year Portland with Bill Walton had won the NBA championship.

They sat in their assigned seats, drank beer, and talked. He didn't remember what they talked about, but they paid little attention to the game, turned to each other instead, engaged in inebriated conversation. He knew the Sonics were losing, however, since everyone was booing.

After the game, Peter had an idea to go to the lounge at the top of the Smith Tower for drinks. An elderly man ran the elevator, an anachronistic service that was still maintained at the Smith Tower for the sake of tradition, once the tallest building west of the Mississippi. Peter imagined that he had maintained this position for decades. The elevator operator was talkative; he talked about the history of the Smith Tower like it was part of his job, like a tour guide.

A guy in a three-piece-suit with his date laughed at the elevator operator, and his date laughed along with him. "We're not interested in your senile view of shit," he said, to the elevator operator, and he and his date laughed again.

"Shut the fuck up," Peter said.

The three-piece-suit guy gaped. "Wha…"

"Shut the fuck up or I'll fucking shut you the fuck up you fucking fuck."

He shut the fuck up, and Peter and Billie smiled warmly at the elevator operator as they exited the elevator in front of the startled three-piece-suit guy and his embarrassed date.

They sat in a booth by the window and looked out at Elliott Bay.

"Wow," Billie said.

"Yeah, what a view, huh?"

"No. What you said to that guy."

"I hate guys like that." Peter was still angry, angry at a world that produced so many assholes. Everywhere, nothing but assholes.

"You're a man."

Peter laughed. "Yes?"

"Yeah—you're a man. I like that." She smiled at him sparkly-eyed.

They resumed their look at the bay and the lights of the city. Across the bay on Alki was his home, wife and kids. Strangely, Peter all of a sudden missed his family.

They talked. They kissed. For the first time, he literally told Billie that he loved her. He told her over and over. She didn't reply. She smiled, drank. They stared at each other, drinking until the bar closed.

All the way to her house he repeated that he loved her. He couldn't stop telling her he loved her. She continued to not reply.

He dropped her off. "I love you," he said, "despite yourself."

She got out, started walking slowly to her door, then turned and ran back, opening the door. "I love you!" she called out then slammed the door in an exclamation point.

-

Friday they were at a bar. She had just turned 20, still not old enough to do legally what she was doing anyway because she looked older. She was never asked for ID. And at 31, Peter felt old too.

She was going to have a party at her house. She wanted him to come, and she wanted him to bring his wife.

"Why."

"I want to meet her."

"Why."

"It would make it easier for me."

"Why."

"I want to see what she's like."

"Why."

"Stop that! You're sounding like a child."

"Why."

"Don't be immature, Peter. You're not immature."

"I could tell you what she's like."

"I want to see for myself. Will you come?"

"Maybe."

"Whatever," she sighed. "Come—don't come, it's all the same to me. You're invited."

———

At the party Peter decided to get drunk. Many of his students were there, and they kept calling him "Mister Placik."

"Peter, goddammit! I'm Peter!"

"You wanna smoke a joint, Mister Peter?"

"No! No! That stuff will rot your brain."

"And that won't?" He nodded at Peter's fourth whiskey/seven.

"All the great American writers drink! Hemingway! Fitzgerald! Faulkner! Wolfe! Algren! Anderson! It's as American as apple pie!"

"But you've had enough," Caitlin said. "You're getting obnoxious."

His response to that of course was to instantly drain the rest of his drink and fetch another. He didn't care. Billie's friends were a bore. The ideals of the sixties were lost on these kids. They were all standing around talking about all the money they were going to make. This was a new generation of determined materialists. They talked of buying houses on Mercer Island and driving

Mercedes', soon as they got their MBAs and went to work for some predatory capitalist corporation that would pay them a generous salary. Everybody was talking about what everybody else did.

Billie introduced him to a friend.

"What do you do?" he said to Peter while shaking his hand.

"I'm a janitor!" Peter bellowed.

"Why did you say that?" Billie said.

"What's wrong with being a janitor! It's a perfectly honorable profession!"

"But you're not a janitor. You're denigrating janitors." She walked off.

Caitlin said, "Why did she talk to you like that?"

"I have no idea! The nerve!"

Later he caught Billie by herself and said, "Your friends are going to set the world on fire."

She frowned at him. "You might be better off if you were more like them."

"Better off! What's better off! Driving a Porsche instead of my perfectly respectable Honda Civic! A yacht perhaps!"

"You're being an asshole." Again, she walked away from him.

Some guy was talking to Peter about himself. He talked about his workouts at the club. He talked about his work in global trade, the next big thing. "The world is shrinking. Japan is going to be the next super power," he said. He kept talking. Peter didn't bother listening.

"I guess there's some correspondence going on here," Peter finally said, "But I don't know what the fuck it is."

The guy kept talking, not even acknowledging Peter's remark.

Peter walked off to get another drink without bothering to excuse himself.

On the ride home, Caitlin wanted to know why Billie hung at his side like a leech all night.

"Did she? I hadn't noticed."

"She couldn't keep her eyes off you." A moment passed, then she said: "I don't like her."

"Oh? Why?"

"Well, for one thing she told somebody when she knew I had to be able to hear was that all she had to do was bat her eyes in order to get an A from you."

"She said that?"

"Yes."

"Well then, she'll be in for a surprise when she sees her grade!"

"Does she do the work?"

"She's brilliant."

"Well then, you have to grade her accordingly."

"What's sad is that she couldn't care less about serious literature."

"Oh?"

"She's doing it for a credit, is all."

"That's too bad."

"Yeah ah well, fuck it."

"You're drunk."

"And she's a bitch! A fucking whore bitch!"

"Good thing I'm driving."

They were driving south across the Aurora Bridge.

"Pull over!" he demanded. "I'm going to jump!"

Caitlin sighed.

The evening had been a fiasco. They shouldn't have gone. Peter had been obnoxious. He didn't like Billie's materialistic friends, and obviously Billie and Caitlin hadn't hit it off.

At school Monday morning Peter said to her: "Let's get away this weekend."

"Where?"

"To the ocean."

"I'd love to. I've never been."

"Okay then."

"But I can't. A friend's coming up from Portland this weekend to stay with me."

"Bring her along; we'll have *un casa de tres!*"

She laughed. "The friend is a guy."

"Never mind then!"

She continued to giggle. "Maybe the following weekend."

"Is this friend a lover?"

"Ex."

"Aha!"

"We're just friends now."

"Caiti wanted to know why you were so friendly with me."

"I'm friendly with everyone."

"Oh?"

"It's what you should have told Caiti."

"I told her it's because women can't leave me alone."

Billie kept being amused; she couldn't stop laughing. "Your wife was jealous?"

"Is that what you want?"

"I don't want anything."

"I apologize for my behavior. I had too much to drink."

"Everyone thought you were funny."

"Well you were a charming host," he said, exchanging one lie with another.

"You should have stayed. It really got going after you left."

"A real orgy, huh?"

"Not quite. But I'm still hungover."

"What did you think of Caiti?"

"I don't know…I guess I expected more."

"More? More of what?"

"Maybe that's not fair."

"You don't know her."

"No, of course not. I just got the impression that all she cares about is you and the kids."

"What's wrong with that?"

"Nothing as far as it goes. I just feel that women should be more ambitious these days. It's no longer the fifties."

"Well, of course you're very different that she is. And you're younger. Maybe your viewpoint will change when you have a family."

"Oh no."

Something was clearly off here. It reinforced his hunch that he shouldn't have brought Caitlin to the party. On the other hand, what possible difference could it make?

They met the following evening for drinks. She seemed nervous and agitated, like he'd never seen her before. He wondered if she was on speed. She was anxiously chomping on gum. She ordered one Irish Coffee after another. She was buzzing like a fly, talking on and on about trite, unspecific topics.

He said: "How was it with your friend?"

"I cooked him this huge special dinner, and we got into a fight."

"What about?"

"I don't remember. Nothing important. The same stupid shit we always fight about. It's one reason why we broke up."

"What's another?"

She shrugged gloomily, and siphoned her drink.

"Are you still in love with him?"

"Are you still in love with your wife?" she shot back.

"Touché."

She shrugged. "Michael's always beating me up emotionally. He says he loves me then he beats me up emotionally."

"That happens."

"With Michael it happens a lot. Sunday he beat me up emotionally, then had the gall to expect sex."

"You're not going to pretend you don't understand that, are you?"

"Understand what? That sex makes it all right? What bullshit! Why do you men use that thing between your legs as a fucking *weapon!*"

Peter went silent. He realized that he now had to accept what he had suspected: She was still in love with this Michael character and had fucked him.

He raged at himself. He had fallen for that old trick of falling in love, leaving himself vulnerable for inevitable heart break. He never seemed to learn.

"I'm sorry," she said. "I'm just bummed tonight."

"It's all right."

She managed a smile.

He said: "I have a feeling you're going to hurt me."

"I'm twenty," she said rhetorically.

"I heard."

She smiled again, warm and tired like. She was burnt out about something.

"You're not in love with me at all," he said.

She looked up with a surprised look. "I don't know. What if I was? What would that accomplish? I won't be your mistress."

"Are we going to the ocean?"

She shrugged. "I don't know…I don't know if I want to have an affair now."

"Well, look, if you want to, let me know."

She nodded and sipped her drink.

"Go to the ocean with me," he said, hating himself for having to beg. "Spend the weekend with me. Then decide."

"Decide," she repeated, weighing the word. "When I'm with you I'm attracted to you sexually. When I'm alone I start thinking about what I'm doing. You're my teacher. You're married. It's inappropriate."

"Go to the ocean with me," he repeated, desperate.

"Okay."

———

The week passed and she was not in class. He tried calling her but she didn't answer. Friday came and he finally got a hold of her.

"Are you ready to leave?"

"Leave?"

"For the ocean."

"The ocean…Oh…I forgot."

"You *forgot*?"

"I've been sick all week, and I haven't been thinking straight."

"Are you all right?"

"Yes. Just a bad cold."

"So, the ocean."

"I don't think I want to go. I'm still a little under the weather."

"Okay."

"Is that okay?"

"Whatever."

"I'll call you later."

She never returned to class. During the following weeks he managed to get over her of course, or get over whatever this absurd feeling was. In just two weeks he went from thinking about her constantly to thinking about her hardly at all. She hadn't turned in that essay about Hemingway. He passed her anyway, as he might any other student he cared little about.

SIXTEEN

Peter had decided to do his final dissertation on F. Scott Fitzgerald, and he needed a hook, some theory about Fitzgerald that had never been presented before. The love/hate/competitive thing between him and Hemingway had already been done *ad infinitum*, as well as the co-dependency and destructiveness between Scott and Zelda, as well as his narcissism and alcoholism. He decided to present the theory that Fitzgerald was dyslexic. He was a notoriously poor speller (as was Hemingway) and never stopped writing "etc." as "ect." his whole life. He also intimated that Scott stole Zelda's prose and used it in his own work, including in *The Great Gatsby*.

It was published but not well received. It was criticized that the insinuation that Fitzgerald was dyslexic and a plagiarist was absurd. But everyone seemed to love what he wrote about Fitzgerald's relationship with Hemingway, the hero worship he provided for Hemingway's fragile ego; the symbolic rivalry between Scott and Zelda that was practically incestuous, since they looked so much like each other, two beautiful blonds. But that could have been picked out of any biography of Fitzgerald, and as such, hardly unique.

He devoted several thousand words to Fitzgerald's narcissism and self-destructiveness. Narcissists don't love themselves, or anyone else. They are always hiding their true selves, presenting false images to compensate, more concerned with how they appear than how they feel, and hide what they believe to be their real selves behind alcoholism or drug use. The board said nothing about that.

83

Jackson was staying at Peter and Caitlin's. He and Josephine were split up again and he had sold his place in Indianola and he needed a place to stay until he could find another house to put a down payment on.

He complained that Josephine spent all day and night at the Kingston Tavern drinking and shooting pool, half the time not coming home at all. He'd had it.

He was the best man at a friend's wedding and still hadn't returned the rental tux. It would be totally out of character for him to go through the motions of returning it, despite the money he'd left as collateral. Caitlin would eventually take it to the Salvation Army, since it was way too small for Peter.

Jackson always had three or four packs of cigarettes lying around half full; he never seemed able to finish an entire pack before opening another. He bought a brand new Schwinn 10-speed bicycle to get around on, since he'd had too many DUI's to risk driving again. He pedaled away one day, returning without it, unable to remember where he'd left it.

Roach was over one day. Peter, Roach, and Jackson were sitting around drinking beer and shooting the shit, and Roach said to Jackson: "Before I forget, Jacky, would you get my sweater you borrowed Friday?" Jackson nodded, "Sure, Roach." Roach waited a moment, then said. "Could you get it for me now, buddy, before I forget and leave without it?" "I won't forget, John, don't worry. Just let me finish this smoke, huh?" Peter and Roach glanced at each other, sensing the obvious: Jackson did not have Roach's sweater. The cigarette was finished, and five minutes later Roach reminded him about the sweater. "I said not to worry, John, I'll have your goddamn sweater before you leave." Roach drained his beer. "I'm leaving now, Jacky." He walked over to the front door and turned to Jackson with his hands on his hips. "Jackson," he said. "Yes, John?" Jackson bounded up to him with a sincere question mark written all over his innocent face, as if he had no idea what Roach wanted. "My sweater?" "Oh sure," he said, then broke into a monologue about nothing that had anything to do with any sweater, about how he was going to hire Roach to do some work on the house he was going to buy, a fix-er-upper he was looking at, because Roach was a master carpenter. "Jackson, we've discussed all that. I have to go now. Could you get my sweater?" "Okay! Okay! I'll get your goddamned sweater! Jesus!" he exclaimed, angry at Roach for making a big production about nothing, running downstairs to his bedroom for a minute and returning without the sweater. He was even angrier now; angry only the way Jackson can be, as if it was anybody and everybody's fault but his own that the sweater was missing. "So what's the problem, Jacky?" Roach inquired. "There's no problem, John, and if there is a problem it's just that I left the sweater at Hoge's...and even if I didn't, they're mass produced and I'll buy you another goddamned sweater." Now Roach was pissed. "That's my favorite sweater, Jackson, and they are *not* mass produced. It's a hundred per cent wool sweater and is *hand made* by a craftsman who sells his goods at the Public Market and I paid over a hundred bucks for it." "Yeah well don't get so uptight, it'll turn up." "How 'bout calling Hoge and see if it's there?" "Yeah!" Jackson said, as if enlightened. He hopped over to the telephone and punched in the number. He talked to Hoge; the sweater wasn't there. Then he called someone else, and the sweater wasn't there either. "It's gotta be somewhere," Roach said. "You're right, John, it's gotta be somewhere, and wherever it is I'll find it, don't worry." So Roach was about to leave, red-faced enraged, and Jackson had his arm around his shoulders. "Don't worry, Roach, we'll get your sweater back, okay?" Roach nodded, downcast, like a little boy who had misplaced his school books, as if he actually *believed* Jackson despite his ominous history, simply because Jackson sounded so damned sincere about it, and furthermore, probably *was* sincere; he probably believed himself that he would find the sweater and return it. Though Roach had to know, at least subconsciously, that his sweater was gone the moment Jackson had slipped it on and walked out of Roach's house. "It's not replaceable, you know, Jacky," Roach lamented. "I've had that sweater for two years, and I'll never find another sweater like it." "I know *exactly* what you're sayin', Roach, "Jackson said, though how could he know, when he had trouble holding onto material possessions for two minutes much less two years, "an' that's why I promise you I'll find your sweater if I have to turn this city upside down." So Roach left, and all was cool between friends.

That afternoon Caitlin found an unfamiliar sweater in the dryer. She couldn't think who it could belong to, since it was too small for Peter and Jackson and she knew it didn't belong to either Thomas or Fitzgerald.

Upstairs she asked Peter and Jackson if they knew anything about it.

"Oh that's right," Jackson said. "It got all muddy so I washed it."

"You washed a wool sweater?" Caitlin said.

"It's wool?"

She handed it to him. He held it up in front of himself. "Oh shit."

———

Jackson always seemed to be loaded. It was downers mostly: Booze, marijuana, barbs, tranquilizers, pain killers—anything to slow down his hyper manic consciousness. He only took uppers to get himself going in the morning, a bennie with a cup of coffee. After that it was vegging out in front of the TV all day and night hardly moving a muscle except to the bathroom or the fridge for a beer. He seemed to depend on the TV as one of his drugs, staring at it hypnotically regardless of the content. Sports was number one on his list—any sport superseded anything else. And football was number one on his list of sports, but it could be Australian rules tiddlywinks, if that's all that was on.

Peter couldn't have any liquor around or it would vanish. It was nothing for him to polish off a fifth of whiskey and a half a rack of beer in one afternoon and act perfectly normal. What annoyed Peter was that Jackson would never buy any booze. If there was no booze in the house, he seemed perfectly content without it.

Peter's lower back had been bothering him for some time, so he finally went to the doctor, who couldn't find anything specifically wrong with his back, but prescribed pain pills. At home he told Caitlin he wasn't going to take the pain pills unless his back was really bothering him, since he hated the side effects from the goddamned things. Fifteen minutes later Jackson was complaining about the stiff neck he woke up with that morning, and asked Peter for one of his pain pills. He gave him one.

That evening about six Jackson was fast asleep on the sofa. Peter called out to him and there wasn't a twitch of a response. He tried shaking him to no avail. Peter got an idea and went to look at his pain pills. Half the prescription was gone.

"Do you think he OD'd?" Peter said to Caitlin, the both of them standing over him in wonder.

"I sincerely hope so," Caitlin said, and walked away.

Peter shrugged and hid the rest of his pain pills.

———

Though Jackson gave them money for room and board, he didn't do anything to help out around the house, and it was getting on Peter and Caitlin's nerves.

He homesteaded himself on the best chair in front of the TV, and that's where he stayed until he went to bed.

So Peter finally told him they would appreciate it if he helped out a little bit around the house. Jackson looked chagrined and agreed to pitch in.

The next morning Peter was awakened by the sound of a lawnmower. He looked out the window and saw Jackson mowing the lawn. Now Peter felt guilty about giving him a bad time about it.

He watched Jackson turn off the mower with the lawn half mowed and go sit down in a lawn chair taking a cigarette break.

There the lawnmower stayed until the next day when Peter finished the mowing, trimming, edging, weeding, and raking while Jackson had planted himself back in front of the TV.

Jackson had an amazing talent for making people accept his behavior, as if they were tolerant of the eccentricities of a complex genius, like Einstein. The only problem was that Jackson displayed no proclivity toward genius, unless it was the genius for laziness and irresponsibility. Nevertheless, everyone tolerated his behavior, friends and family alike. They tolerated his frittering away money that wasn't his, wrecking borrowed cars, losing borrowed clothes, drinking and drugging himself unconscious—simply due to his talent for ostensibly needing the slack.

———

Then Jackson came home one day and announced that he had applied to Shadel Hospital's Schick program for the control of drinking. It was a conditioned response therapy, he explained. They administered a drug along with the patient's favorite alcoholic beverage, which made the patient violently ill. They would be allowed to drink as much as they liked, as long as they took the drug that made them sick along with it. On alternative days they were to receive therapy and counseling.

The next day Peter drove him to the hospital.

He showed up at Peter and Caitlin's two weeks later with a buddy from the hospital.

"What are you doing here?" Caitlin said. "Did you quit the program?"

"Not at all. We just decided to go AWOL for the day."

"AWOL!"

"Yeah, those four walls were driving us batty. We had to get way for a few hours, right, Raymond?" he said to his friend.

The friend nodded diffidently.

"Are you drinking?"

He made a sick face and shook his head adamantly. "Drinking is the last thing on our minds, right, Raymond?"

Raymond continued to nod with some expression of doubt.

"But now smoking." Jackson dug into his jeans pocket and brought out a baggy of marijuana. "Oh, Peter!" he said, after rolling a joint and sticking it into his mouth. "One of the things we are supposed to do is make amends to those we have loved and trusted. I have some confessions to make."

"Oh?" Peter said.

"Remember that time you and Caiti got back from vacation and all your marijuana plants were ripped out of your back yard?"

"Yeah..." Peter said, vaguely remembering.

"That was me."

"No shit."

"And remember that time we came out of that bar in Burien and the windshield wipers on your VW bug were torn off?"

"I do."

"That was probably because some kids had given me money to buy them beer and I didn't; I just kept the money."

"Jesus, Jacky. Anything else?"

"Well...there was the time..."

"You know, never mind, I don't want to know."

———

Two weeks later he had graduated with flying colors from Schick and was back staying with Peter and Caitlin. The next day they noticed that a bottle of McNaughton's was missing.

That afternoon Jackson arrived home showing off some new duds he had bought. "The new sober me," he said, then to Peter: "Hey, Peter, I owe you a bottle of whiskey."

"What?"

"I don't know what came over me, but yesterday I had this overwhelming desire to get drunk. Sorry."

"Jacky," Caitlin said, frustrated and confused. "How much you spend on that program at Schick?"

"Three thousand, but no worries, they give refresher courses for free. I'm turning myself back in tomorrow."

He gave Peter the money for the bottle of whiskey, and left, presumably to drink.

———

Two weeks later he returned having completed his refresher course, announcing himself cured—again. "Man—I can't imagine myself ever drinking again. No way, man."

Monday Peter arrived home from classes to find Caitlin lying on the sofa with both boys asleep with her, a forearm across her brow. The boys were getting too big for this arrangement; they looked like two large lumps of cement weighing her down. So he joined them, getting on top. The boys intoned in unison: "Daddy!"

Caitlin moaned.

"You okay?" He jumped off.

"I have a headache."

"Did you take some aspirin?"

"Yes, and I also kicked Jacky out. That should help."

"Oh? Why?"

"He was drunk."

SEVENTEEN

Peter obtained a professor's aid position at the University of Washington. Perry worked for an architectural firm in Bellevue. Paul rented a warehouse in the Soho district where he made and sold his furniture. They were all married, having kids, buying houses, and living the American Dream. Ronald Reagan was president, and the wealth was trickling down—on the three Placik brothers anyway.

Thomas and Fitzgerald were growing like weeds, and would eventually shoot past their father. They got excellent grades and were good at sports. Peter took them to the tennis club and taught them tennis. Fitz would eventually be the number one seed on the University of Washington tennis team.

Peter had become a bourgeoisie. The family abided in familial bliss. Caitlin continued to ignore Peter's serial trysts with his students.

At the tennis club, after tennis he worked out on the nautilus. Right next to the nautilus equipment was the only international squash court in the club. When he worked out there was oftentimes a young woman who played squash. She was very athletic and extremely dedicated to the game, diving for shots that were obviously out of reach. Peter knew next to nothing about squash, but she seemed very good at it, and always played with men, especially one man in particular. She had an interesting, unmade up face, short blonde hair, a body curved tight with lean muscles. She was not unpleasant to look at, and between points she spotted him looking at her, smiling in return.

So Peter continued to gaze admiringly at her between sets on the nautilus, and she would return the look engagingly between shots. The man with whom she played noted this visual exchange.

Peter was in the club bar one night with one of his tennis partners when she rushed in and sat down across from this man with whom she usually played, her head dripping from the shower.

"They're having an affair," Howard, his tennis partner said, noting Peter's interest.

"Oh?"

"Yes, it's the club scandal. His wife it seems is very tolerant. He has quite the reputation. He's fucked half the wives at the club, it seems."

"Is she married too?"

"I don't know, but I'm envious of the bastard."

"Hm," Peter agreed, nodding.

The Casanova in question was nothing spectacular to look at, mid-forties, medium height, average looks. Yet her attention was focused squarely on him. She talked and he listened. He sensed Peter and Howard looking at them, and he glanced over. She didn't seem to notice the attention.

"Ah, well," Peter said.

"Yes," Howard said. "What a waste."

———

He was walking out to his vehicle in the parking lot later, and he spotted her putting her gear away in the trunk of a Volvo station wagon. He said: "Hello there."

She looked up, a bit startled, and said hello back.

One day as he finished with a set of bench presses, he sat up and there she was directly in front of him, toweling off, her blond hair soiled with sweat, her muscular body drenched. Her opponent had left somewhere. Peter said, "How's the match going?"

"It's going all right," she said, accenting her speech with what Peter recognized as British. "I'm winning, though I don't know how. Ralph is the best squash player in the club."

The best squash player in the club returned. He looked at her questionably, ignoring Peter.

"Sandy Clinch," she said to Peter, extending her right hand.

"Peter Placik," Peter returned, taking it.

"And this is Ralph Lloyd."

Ralph Lloyd nodded without a smile, then entered the squash court to finish their match.

Sandy Clinch shrugged at Peter with a smile, and followed him in.

In the shower later Peter witnessed what ostensibly made Ralph Lloyd so popular with the ladies of the club. He caught Peter's astonished stare, and smiled smugly, displaying eight or nine thick facile inches.

In the lobby turning in their locker keys, Sandy left Ralph Lloyd and walked up to Peter. She said: "I've watched your tennis game. You're very good."

"Thank you, but you're being generous."

"You're impressive on the nautilus equipment as well." She smiled.

He smiled back. "Do you play tennis?"

"Used to. Do you play squash?"

"Oh, no."

"Well then, bugger it, would you like to fetch a drink?"

Ralph Lloyd watched with open-mouthed astonishment as they walked away from him towards the bar.

"Mister Lloyd doesn't look pleased," Peter said.

"Yes, well, stuff him."

Lover's spat?

She and Ralph Lloyd were both from England, recruited by Boeing as engineers. This was coincidental, however, since it was here at the club where they met. "He's very smart," she said, as if this had relevance to anything.

She actually had a brief career as a professional tennis player, she said. She played at Wimbledon when she was sixteen, losing in the second round to Martina Navratilova. Then she contacted toxic shock syndrome and was bed-ridden for two years. When she recovered enough to get back on the court, her father handed her a squash racket, since she was too weak as yet to pick up a tennis racket, and the strokes were so similar. She'd been playing ever since.

Peter asked if she wanted to play tennis sometime, and she said she would love to, but that he would have to be patient with her because she hadn't played in years.

They made a date for Saturday at ten a.m. at the club.

———

It was obvious by her strokes that she knew the game, though she had a tendency toward a squash stroke, resulting in too much underspin. And though she was rusty, she was of course in excellent shape, and they had a decent match, Peter winning 6-4, 6-2.

Afterwards, he asked her if he could buy her lunch. She said she'd love to, but had another commitment. "Another time?"

"All right."

"Are you married?"

"Yes."

"I knew it."

"Oh?"

"I could tell. You're…tentative…I guess is the word, not so full of yourself like the other blokes at the club."

"I guess that's a compliment."

"It is, yes, it is. You don't come on like a Billy goat—all horns."

"But I'm married."

She shrugged. "Right. All the decent chaps are."

"Then we'll still have lunch."

"You see, Peter, I've been hurt rather badly by another married man, and I imagine women fall in love with you all the time."

"I hear it's Ralph Lloyd who's the Don Juan of the club."

"Oh, Ralph is one of those blokes who's full of himself."

Peter assumed it was Ralph Lloyd who hurt her "rather badly".

He said, "I knew the first time I saw you I wanted to get to know you."

They strolled out to the parking lot in the Seattle mist.

She was kicking her racket playfully with every other step. "I knew the first time I saw you doing those pull-ups or dips or whatever you do with that equipment that you were trouble…You know—this isn't the first time we've met."

"Huh? You mean before we met here at the club?"

"Yes. We met once before. You don't remember?"

"No!"

"Think about it."

She kissed him goodbye on the cheek.

Driving home, he tried to remember where he could have met her, but couldn't think. Had they had sex on one of his drunken nights out?

———

The next Saturday afternoon after tennis she agreed to go into the bar. After two whiskeys, he began to get unhinged, and admitted to her that he had had affairs.

"What's your wife like?"

"She's beautiful, a wonderful mother, intelligent."

"Right. I can see why you shag about then."

He laughed, but she didn't laugh back.

"She must be amazingly tolerant."

"I think we both are."

"What's that?"

"Let's hear more about you."

She was only 24, which was surprising to him, since she'd had numerous relationships, as she told him all about these strange relationships she'd had with really fucked-up men. But then, people are fucked-up in general, aren't they? she said, and therefore not much different as lovers. Men as lovers are so much different when described by women as they are when described by men.

"And Ralph Lloyd?"

"Ah, Ralph's not strange at all, just a regular bloke with a huge dick, more than I can handle really."

Peter shook his head and laughed.

She was perceptive to a degree that Peter found eerie. She told him all about himself, and how could she know all this? She said it was this certain skill she innately possessed, delineating character from the moment she met someone. It was why she was reluctant to get involved with him. "You don't remember where it was we met, do you?"

"I confess I don't."

"I'll give you another hint: Another of my hobbies is rock climbing."

Peter shrugged, still clueless.

"We met on a hike up into Lake Ingalls. You were with a pretty brunette, which I assume was not your wife."

"That was a few years ago. You must have been very young."

"Nineteen. I hadn't moved here yet, but I knew I would eventually. This Northwest of yours is a paradise. I was traveling with some British mates."

"It's coming back to me now. We were resting and you passed us by."

"Yes. Oh sod it, let's go."

"Go?"

"Yes, go. It's a shag we want, isn't it?"

———

The next week she left for a week's vacation in the Bahamas with a friend, a female friend, she added. She wrote him a letter addressed care of the club while she was there. She said she was playing tennis every day and planned on beating him when she returned. She was running along the white sand at sunset every evening. She was learning to scuba dive and surf. She said she missed him.

She called him at his office at the university when she got back. She said she wouldn't be able to play tennis for awhile. She had stepped on some sea urchins while scuba diving which had impaled themselves in her foot, and which were still there.

"Still where? In your foot?"

"I know, bloody gross, huh? A bloke killed them by pouring boiling wax on them. He said he could also kill them by peeing on them, but I opted for the boiling wax, which bloody hurt, but which apparently suffocates them."

"But how do you get them out?"

"Apparently they eventually work themselves out, the little buggers."

They met downtown at Mama's Mexican restaurant. They had margaritas before dinner, Dos Equis with their tamales, beans, rice, and chicken enchiladas, and Mexican coffees after eating. They drank their coffee liqueurs down and ordered two more.

"What do you think of me?" she said.

"I think you're a superior athlete, in and out of bed."

She laughed. "And?"

"And cute as a bug's butt to boot."

"To 'boot'? I'm unfamiliar with that term."

"It means 'as well' 'too' 'also'."

"To boot. Bloody odd expression."

"I guess it is, come to think of it. Wonder where it came from."

"Go on then."

"You have a fantastic ass."

She shook her head and sighed. "Bubble butt."

He laughed. "No."

The Mexican coffees were soaring through them like *conquistadores*, triumphantly, succeeding in their inebriated manic quest. Peter felt inspired and confrontational.

She said: "You're bloody attractive."

"You're just trying to get me into the sack."

"I've already succeeded in that endeavor."

They laughed.

"You have the best body I've ever seen."

"Oh, come on."

"I'm serious. I suppose women use you this way."

"Not enough."

"Oh come on, you're just an old romantic. I know you're capable of falling head over heels without watching where you're going. You're not like Ralph at all. On the other hand, you do cheat on your wife."

"You are the perceptive one."

"I'm serious."

"And I'm not." He turned his smile upside down.

She laughed. "You bastard."

"Now you're turning me on."

He drove her home. Like the gentleman she thought he was, he walked her to her door. She asked him in.

"You sure? It is a work night, after all."

She nodded without hesitation. "Come on in, Romeo."

They stumbled straight to bed. He lifted her up into his arms and tossed her onto the bed.

"Oh, Tarzan!" she said.

———

He called her the next day and asked if they could get together the coming weekend. She said to call her Saturday morning.

He called her Saturday morning as requested and there was no answer. He called her several times throughout the day and she never answered. *What the fuck?* Peter pondered.

Angry, he went out drinking. He went into a bar in Ballard where there was live music and dancing. He danced with a chubby young blonde whose name was Dini, or Dana, he couldn't remember which. She was local and had striking black eyes. He asked to go home with her, and she hesitated a nanosecond.

———

Monday morning he called Sandy at her work. "You didn't answer your phone Saturday."

"No."

"Why not?"

"I don't know."

"You don't *know?*"

"Are you angry?"

"Do you want me to be angry?"

"I do like you. I guess I have a funny way of showing it then, don't I?"

"Hilarious. I laughed my ass off every time I called and you didn't answer the goddamned phone!"

"I was with Ralph, to tell you the truth."

"Ah."

"We had some things to tidy up."

"I see."

"Look, I'm really busy. Can we meet for a drink tonight?"

They met at the J&M Café downtown on First Avenue.

"So, what did you end up doing Saturday night?"

"I went out and got laid."

"I figured you'd do that."

"I would have preferred being with you."

"Peter the romantic." She took a small sip of scotch. "I knew that you would be upset with me and it wouldn't be much for you to go out and meet someone. You're very good looking after all, and charming in your way."

"Don't patronize me."

She stared into her drink. "I should have answered the phone. I'm sorry."

"So what's with you and Ralph?"

"He's in a tizzy about you, as if he has a right. He's stringing half a dozen women along as it is."

"I see. You're using me to get back at him."

"Maybe there's some of that. But I do like you."

They drank their whiskeys and ordered two more.

"We'll leave it at that then," he said.

"At what?"

"We like each other. We like fucking each other. We'll leave it at that."

"And Ralph?"

"Ralph is your business, obviously."

"Right. I'm involved with two married men then."

They drank.

"I do fancy you, Peter."

"We've established that."

"You're going to think I'm silly."

"Too late: I already do."

She laughed. The whiskey was having its intended effect. "I mean, I *have* taken a fancy to you and I'm worried that I'll fall in love with you. I'm not sure about you. I have a gut feeling about you that I can't shake."

"Okay," he said, without asking her to elaborate.

"I'm just getting over Ralph as it is."

He nodded. "Men can be real assholes, can't they?"

"You're not angry anymore?"

"If you're hung up on Ralph, there's not much I can do about that."

"I'm not hung up on him. I'm pretty much over the wanker by now. But it hurt, and I don't want to go through it again. Not with a married man."

"I'm sorry I don't have any written guarantees. I'm just playing out my feelings." He shrugged. "If you don't want to see me, I'll accept that gracefully."

"You're a placid bloke, I'll give you that. Don't you know the rules of this game? It's as old as Adam and Eve. You're supposed to chase me, and I'm supposed to play hard to get."

"I don't play that game or any other."

"I don't imagine you do."

"Are we getting anywhere?"

"I don't know. Are we?"

"It all boils down to this: Are we going to have a relationship or not?"

"And if it is, is it going to be a trusting, solid relationship, or a sordid affair?"

He stared at her thoughtfully, and said: "What was it with Ralph?"

"Oh, sordid all the way. When I'm feeling strongly for someone I have to look before I leap."

He nodded. "Well, Sandy, I think maybe we should just be tennis buddies for awhile."

She gave him a sad, inquiring look of something passing on, or arriving. "All right."

"We can do that, can't we? Be friends, play tennis, go for the occasional drink?"

"And the occasional shag as well?"

"Why not?"

She shrugged. Outside it had become dark. The air was unkind, harsh and biting. They shivered and kissed goodbye.

———

He lost touch with her. She quit coming to the club. A couple years later he saw her while he was stretching getting ready to run the Seattle Marathon. She jogged past him up and down the street. She saw him and waved at him as if they had seen each other just the other day. Her beautiful ass had shrunk to nothing. Very sad.

EIGHTEEN

Caitlin and the boys and Caitlin's 14-year-old cousin Lindsey had already left for Roche Harbor in the San Juan Islands where they were to be staying one week in a rental cabin on the water. Peter was scheduled to leave the following day with his brother Paul and Paul's girlfriend, Jessica.

So he decided to go out and enjoy his one night of freedom.

He walked over to a new bar on Alki close to his house and drank three quick, thirst-quenching beers. He was pleasantly light-headed when she strutted exuberantly in out of the misty rain and sat right next to him. It was interesting how she did this, as if he was already an acquaintance of hers with whom she could casually pick up where they had left off.

"So, ya buyin' me a beer or what?" She draped her raincoat over the back of the bar stool. A beige t-shirt clung to firm braless breasts, brown jeans tight against a round half moon behind, and beat up sneakers. Her reddish brown hair was long, a brilliant thick wave, her face splattered with brown freckles. "You're pretty," she added, smiling.

Peter ordered two more beers.

"That's it?" he said. "Pretty?"

"What's wrong with pretty? Wanna shoot some pool?"

"I hate pool."

"Me too."

"Then why'd you ask me to play?"

She shrugged. "Somethin' to say, I s'ppose."

They introduced each other. Her name was Jane. They talked and lost count of the beers consumed. They stood arm in arm out to her car.

"How old are you?" she said, as if suddenly this was of prime importance. Peter looked at his watch. "In five minutes I will be 39."

"Really?" she said, smiling in celebration. "Happy bee-day!" She leaned over from the driver's seat and gave him a kiss. "You don't look 39—though you don't look 29 either…So…where we headed?"

"Your place."

She said, "It's prob'ly what I need," and proceeded to tell him about this guy she'd been dating and hadn't decided whether she liked him or not.

They drove to her apartment, about a mile up the hill off Admiral Way. Inside while she was in the bathroom, he took a look around and complimented her on her décor when she exited from the bathroom.

"So you gonna feed me bullshit about my piece of shit place or we gonna get it on?"

Afterwards she stared into him intensely with her nervous blue eyes.

"What?" he said.

She reached across him and grabbed a wallet sized photo off the bed stand and held it out to him. It was of a handsome young man with black hair and goatee.

"Good looking dude," Peter said.

"Isn't he?" she said warmly, smiling proudly at the photo.

"So?" He shrugged.

"So…I've been seeing him for a month, and we haven't been to bed yet."

"Ah."

"I mean—obviously I'm attracted to him, you can see for yourself why, and I feel some obligation to him even though he hasn't made a move on me yet for some reason. Also, I just don't do one night stands."

"Yeah," but thinking to himself: Women.

They made love again.

———

He awoke at six a.m. Paul was supposed to pick him up at seven. He jumped up, hurriedly dressed, copied down Jane's phone number, slipping the piece of paper into his wallet, kissed her awake and said he would call. She mumbled an okay and turned over.

He jogged home and quickly stuffed his gear into his duffel bag, grabbed a quick shower, brushed his teeth, and rinsed his rancid mouth out with mouthwash.

And Paul was late. Paul was always late. Why hadn't he counted on that inevitability? He had all the time in the world.

He read the paper with a cup of coffee.

Paul arrived with his girlfriend Jessica, complaining that the bridge was up. Paul always had an excuse why he was late.

Paul had a different girlfriend every time he saw him, but they always had one similar characteristic: They were never Caucasian. Jessica was Samoan.

The ride to the Anacortes ferry took about an hour. They got in line at the ferry, which didn't come for an hour, so they strolled over to a restaurant for breakfast.

Peter got the strangest feeling that Jessica was flirting with him. She was being inappropriately friendly with him at any rate, all piercing brown-eyed smiles, and she kept a monologue going throughout breakfast that neither Peter or Paul seemed much interested in, as though to impress Peter, the college professor, with her intellect, which was young and naïve. She displayed to Peter the book that she was reading: Sartre's *Nausea*. Paul rolled his eyes and stuck his finger in his mouth to simulate vomiting. Peter laughed, mouth crammed full of scrambled eggs. While Paul wasn't looking, she flashed a Lauren Bacall snide smile. As they walked out of the restaurant, she brushed one of her huge breasts against his right forearm. Peter was uncomfortable.

The ferry ride took about an hour and a half. It was July 15, Peter's birthday, which Paul had yet to comment on. There wasn't a cloud in sight, and the water sparkled like a blue prism. They watched the small green islands float past. Boats spotted the blue bay like distant logs. There was a warm comforting breeze. It was quiet and peaceful. Peter leaned over the railing and looked over at Jessica, who looked back, pressing her formidable breasts against the railing and extending her impressive ass.

They got off the ferry at Friday Harbor. The drive from there to Roche Harbor took about twenty minutes.

They met Caitlin and the boys, and Peter and Paul's parents, and Caitlin's cousin Lindsey at the log cabin they were renting. It was old and beautiful and rustic with a broad view of the harbor.

The boys watched Peter lace up his running shoes.

"Can we go with you, Dad?" Fitzgerald said.

"Can you keep up?"

"Yes!" Both boys intoned eagerly.

"Are you going for a run?" Jessica said.

"Yes."

"Can I go, too?"

"Do you run?"

"Like the wind."

"Goddammit, Jessica," Paul said. "you don't run!"

Jessica shrugged with disappointment, and Peter took off with the boys.

They returned half an hour later laughing about one thing or the other.

At six p.m. Peter celebrated his 39th birthday by opening a bottle of McNaughton's. "Happy birthday, me!"

"Has anyone wished you a happy birthday yet?" Caitlin said. It apparently had slipped her mind as well.

"No!"

"Happy birthday, Peter!" everyone suddenly exclaimed, all celebratory smiles.

And then Perry and his crazy girlfriend Lynn arrived. Lynn was one of those eccentrics one meets on occasion in which housework is not in ones daily repertoire. Her home had a flea-bitten path carved from the front door to couch to kitchen to bathroom to bedroom, the sides of which are dusty hillsides of mildewed, rotting junk. You open the stove door to encounter rat turds, the solution of which naturally are cats, who use her house as kitty litter, allowing for the perpetual stench of acidic urine and moldy feces. The relationship baffled everyone. And she wasn't even physically attractive. If you looked hard, a cute girl was buried in there somewhere within the deep wrinkles stretching across her face, cross-hatched with other wrinkled tributaries like an old fisherman. She was a sun worshipper. She was 37.

They had dinner at the restaurant to celebrate Peter's birthday, of which the old man picked up the $200 dollar tab and wouldn't let anyone else pay a cent, even though he made about half the income of each of his sons. Peter's mom sighed in frustration because he was always doing that, and couldn't afford to do that, and the old man's prodigious drinking didn't help matters.

The brothers were talking about the Sonics, who were expected to have a competitive team this year.

"Who gives a shit about a bunch of jungle bunnies with pituitary disorders!" cried the drunken old man, and Jessica gasped.

"Jesus Christ, you old drunken Pollack," Paul said. "Are you ever going to stop being a goddamned racist?"

"It's too late for that," Mom said.

In the morning Peter, Thomas, Fitz, and Perry went to play tennis before breakfast. Peter teamed with Thomas and beat Perry and Fitz, 6-4, 7-5. Then they returned to the cabin for breakfast.

At the breakfast table Peter couldn't stop thinking about this disgusting pedophilic crush he was developing on Lindsey. She'd had her share of adolescent troubles: She had been on drugs, been a runaway, and apparently had been abused by her step-father; the exact sort of abuse not fully defined but had some sexual context to it. So presently she was staying with Caitlin's parents, but was having issues with them as well. Caitlin was talking of having her stay with them for awhile, which Peter obviously didn't think was a good idea. Having a raven-haired, black-eyed teenage beauty with a luridly perfect body move in with a dirty old man and two pubescent teenagers was not smart.

Peter and his mother went for a walk into the woods. They were talking and paying no attention to where they were going; they just wandered off onto one trail after another. They were being adventurous and foolish. Peter's mother at 62 did adventurous and foolish things. She was five-foot-three and oftentimes at home took off on trails like a seven-foot Peter the Great. On weekends, she would have had it with her drunken husband and drive up to the mountains and hike the trails alone. She was healthy, assertive, and liberated.

They paused in their hike and had a lunch of crackers and cheese, carrot sticks and apple slices.

Peter's mother told him she was thinking of moving into her own apartment. She was tired of his father's drunken fishing trips with all his racist drunken friends and coming home all sick and hungover.

"I'm surprised you hadn't before now," Peter said sadly.

"I hung in there because of you boys. If it wasn't because of you boys I would have been long gone."

"I don't know what to say, mom."

"Don't think I haven't been aware of his being with other women, too."

Peter remained silent. He didn't know what to say. She'd never talked like this before. The Placik's never talked.

They carried on with their aimless trek. They exited a trail and found themselves about 200 yards from the cabin. It seemed they had been hiking through a maze. Peter blamed his mother for his own lack of direction. Peter's dad however, had a sixth sense for it. He could close his eyes and spin on a top and then point north, south, east and west like a blood hound. It was uncanny.

———

Later, Peter and Lindsey lay on a hill in front of the cabin, and she drew pictures of the harbor with the sailboats and thick Douglas fir, red Madrona trees sprouting from the hillsides toward the bay. Peter was impressed; they were very good. She wrote poetry, and wrote a spontaneous poem and held it out to Peter. The free verse poem was nowhere as good as her drawing, but it had a lot of feeling to it, a Saxton-like confessional poem of teenage angst.

After he read the poem he looked at her and she was looking back at him with her wide round mythic eyes, misty with love. He became overwhelmed with lust for her, her long soulful body and her long thick hair with its blackberry sheen and her violet eyes which carried eons of mysterious seduction and her sensual Liz Taylor eyebrows and eyelashes. He couldn't stop himself; who could? She was a beautiful nymph; it wasn't his fault. She was all black and bewitching, and he was Humbert Humbert.

Peter was in a dizzy lust daze all afternoon. He tried to burn it off with a four mile, six-minute mile run with Perry. He was obsessed with this fourteen year old girl who was his wife's cousin. He was frightened. What the fuck was he doing!

———

The next morning at nine a.m. they packed their gear in a hasty attempt to make the ten a.m. ferry. He, Caitlin, Lindsey, and the two boys were stuffed into the little brown Honda Civic like compressed rags. He turned to the back seat to observe Lindsey sandwiched between the boys, her beautiful face looking back at him moon-eyed. Seventeen-year-old Thomas was looking out the side window, bored stiff. He ignored Lindsey's flirtations, as if she were too young for him. Fourteen-year-old Fitz looked out the other window, red-faced. He was terrified of Lindsay. There was irony spilling out everywhere.

When they got home and unpacked, Peter took a short nap then got up and went for a run. He ran frantic, lust releasing six-minute miles. He stopped at a phone booth and called Jane. Though it was two in the afternoon, he had woken her up. She didn't know who it was at first. When she realized who it was, she was nonplussed; she hadn't expected to ever hear from him again, which he didn't understand, since he *told* her he would call.

Women are weird, he thought.

They made a date for drinks later.

But later Caitlin wanted to go out to dinner. He tried to talk her out of it, but she was steadfast. So he had to call and postpone his date with Jane till the following evening. She said: "That figures."

Caitlin and Peter went out to dinner and came home early. They were fighting, which annoyed him because he had planned on having sex, and she never had sex with him when they were fighting, for some reason he could not comprehend. What better way to make up from a fight than with sex? So instead he became even more sullen and agitated.

At ten he told Caitlin he was going for a run. She shrugged, "Whatever." He ran to a phone booth and called Jane. She wasn't home, or didn't answer.

At noon the next day, he went for a run and stopped at this same phone booth and called Jane. He woke her up again. The woman was always sleeping. He asked her if she felt like going to a ride up to Snoqualmie Pass. She laughed and said "No, think of something else to do." She yawned loudly into the phone.

"Okay…um…How 'bout let's ride out to the U-district and walk around on campus…or maybe Volunteer Park or the zoo, perhaps the waterfront and the market…There's all sorts of things we can do."

She laughed. "You're weird. Why do we have to go anywhere?" she said, yawning again. "Want some coffee?"

So he jogged over to her house and they had two cups of coffee each and she went off on this long rambling monologue about this same guy she was seeing, and then they went to bed.

And then there was post-sex turbulence. She asked him to take her to dinner later, and he replied that he didn't want to spend the money.

"So you're quite willing to take me on silly rides in your silly little car but you won't spend forty bucks for a meal?"

"I've got a wife, two kids, and a mortgage."

"Oh, don't give me that shit. You're a college professor. I know guys who make hardly anything and wouldn't hesitate to take me to dinner."

"Tenure."

"Huh?"

"I don't have tenure. I don't make the money you apparently think I do. I made more money when I was in the sheet metal worker's union."

"What do you make?"

"Thirty-five thousand."

"Thirty-five thousand! You're a millionaire compared to what I make!"

"It doesn't seem like a lot after I've paid the bills."

"So tell me about yourself. I know nothing 'bout you 'cept you're married with children and make thirty-five thousand a year as a college professor, so you say."

"I'm six-foot-two and weigh 180. I play tennis, lift weights and run. I read everything, including the back of cereal boxes. I'm writing a novel. I vote Democrat…"

"Tha's enough for now," she said, yawning. She sighed. They kissed and made up. They made love.

Then he got a bright idea for a joke. He jumped out of bed suddenly. "I'm leaving!"

She sat up, startled. "That figures."

He laughed and got back into bed with her and tried to hug her but she shoved him away. "Don't touch me!"

"Hey! I was only going to say that I have to run a coupla errands then I'll be back to take you out to dinner."

She sneaked an uncertain look at him. She smiled.

They kissed and made up again.

"We've known each other two days and we're acting like old, worn out lovers."

"I know," she said. "It's my fault."

He thought so too. He left. He wondered what he was doing, wasting his time with the petty emotions of a neurotic. But he didn't dislike her. He liked her long reddish/brown hair and blue eyes and tight little body with her almost perfect breasts. The splash of freckles on her face only seemed to add to her refreshing uniqueness. But frankly, there weren't many women he did dislike. It was ironic, in a way. He walked down the busy streets and said to himself one after another, "I would with her...I would with her...I would with her...I would with her...Okay, maybe not her..."

Later he told Caitlin he was going out to campus for a pick-up basketball game,

and left.

Back at Jane's, she made the announcement she didn't want to go to dinner. *Oh shit*, he thought. *Here we go again.* "Why not."

"'cause you don't want to spend the money."

"Yes, I do! I want to spend all my *money!*"

"See? You don't. You're cheap."

"Oh, fuck."

They sat and had a beer. What they decided to do was walk up to the Thriftway, and he would buy some steaks and wine, and she would cook him dinner. She said it's what she wanted to do.

So it's what they did.

They drank the wine, ate the steaks with salad and baked potato and watched part of an old movie which they paid scant attention to because they were tipsy from wine and horny, and before they knew it they were on it on the couch and he came right away, and apologized, and she said it was all right, they had all night. She was drinking wine and chattering away and he fell asleep.

———

109

He woke and wondered where he was. He looked at his watch. Six. Oh shit. What would he tell Caitlin this time?

He got dressed and didn't see Jane. There was a note on the kitchen table. "Sorry. I'm not used to going to bed so early. Going out drinking."

The note annoyed him, but he shrugged his annoyance away. He had more pressing worries.

He found Caitlin wide awake on the sofa. She asked him where he'd been.

"Ah, shit, we had too many beers after playing ball so I decided to spend the night with a colleague rather than drive home."

"Why didn't you call?"

"Too drunk to think about it."

"Think you drink too much?"

"Perhaps."

Her face contorted to misshapen tremors, then exploded with tears.

He sat down beside her and hugged her. She pushed him away. "Leave me alone!"

He did love Caitlin. But right now he was obsessed with this pubescent and needed to get her out of his mind before he got into trouble. The definitions and degrees of love were so subjective and ambiguous they were impossible to define. People need to be loved more than they need to love. Maybe love was nothing more than food for our self-survival. He was obsessed with Lindsey and terrified of what he might do about it. Caitlin was possessed and possessive. She was his—in his head—for always. He wasn't good for her, but she was perfect for him. But that was irrelevant, and another novel…Caitlin was beautiful, but Lindsey was divine. She was Juliet, Beatrice, Lolita, Venus…But of course it was a fantasy, because he could never have her. She was fourteen for God's sake! But so what, Lolita was twelve. Poe's wife was thirteen. Jerry Lee Lewis and Elvis fell in love and married thirteen-year-olds. Juliet was twelve, Dante's Beatrice eleven! And Lindsey *looked* like a woman. She acted fourteen, however, because she *was* fourteen, and he realized that whatever it was she felt for him was nothing more than an adolescent infatuation adolescents felt for innumerous people from their peers to their teachers…And God only knows what abuse had already been rendered to that delicate psyche…And then there was Jane, a surrogate, who looked great too, though could not be compared to the stunning Elizabeth Taylor beauty of Lindsey. Also, Jane didn't even have a

job at the moment, collecting unemployment; she seemed to have no construc-
tive interests or hobbies; she drank too much and spent too much time in bars
and slept her life away. Yet somehow she radiated character and unpretentious
splendor and seemed genuinely sincere, honest, and sentimental—and was fun.
But she was a neurotic; she was too emotional and intense.

Sometimes a strange set of circumstances fall into place for the sake of
fate. Caitlin was gone with the boys, and he and Lindsey were in the house
alone.

Oh shit.

Peter was sitting on the sofa, reading *Solo Faces*. Lindsey collapsed on the
sofa beside him, her small behind bouncing off the cushion like on a trampo-
line. She said:

"I got something in my eye.

"Let's see," he said. "Which one?"

"Either one." She raised her face to him.

He laughed and looked at each eye. She kissed him suddenly. He returned
it. She pushed her tongue into his mouth. He pushed her away.

"Lindsey…"

"What?"

"You're a virgin."

"Who, me? Hell no!"

She kissed him again. He kissed her back, then suddenly pushed her away
again.

He rushed to his room, changed into his running gear, and dashed out the
door.

He ran south along Alki Avenue, past the old charming beach cottages and
the condos that were suddenly sprouting like a blight. He pushed himself hard,
running about six-minute miles.

He had been falling into a "mood." He could tell when it was happening,
like a dark shroud enveloping him. He could not handle this mood without running. He's not sure he could write if not for running. The truth that was inside
of him could only be out on paper by running. Running was a solitary pursuit.
So was writing. And right now he needed to be alone with his thoughts. He
needed to flee. He needed to hide within his conscious. What was he doing? She
was fourteen. She acted like fourteen. She wrote poetry like a fourteen-year-old.

But she looked twenty, a beautiful, perfect twenty. He turned right up the long steep Ferry Street, tall Doug fir and thick Alder on each side of him. He came behind West Seattle High School, turned right on California Avenue, then left down Admiral, and home.

———

The next day she acted aloof. She avoided him.

"Lindsey—I apologize for yesterday. It was wrong of me."

She didn't respond.

He sat down in a lawn chair in the back yard. He was re-reading Nabokov's *Lolita*. She snatched the book out of his hands, read the back cover, looked at him with disgust and dropped it back in his lap.

Later in the day Perry rode up in his ten-speed with his tennis racket in his back pack and asked Peter to hit.

Before they left for tennis, they sat in the back yard and had a beer.

Lindsey appeared in front of them and started flirting with Perry. She picked cherries off the cherry tree, stood before him and tossed them at his mouth. For awhile he was catching a few in his mouth and spitting out the seeds. But then she increased her cadence and he couldn't keep up. They were laughing as he attempted to fend off the onslaught. Peter was not amused.

The Placik brothers jumped on their bikes and rode to the tennis court. Peter took his frustration out on the tennis ball, hitting so hard the balls sailed long. On one overhead smash he hit Perry in the right thigh, leaving a red welt.

Perry glared at him. "Was that necessary?"

"Sorry, Perry."

"What the hell's wrong with you today?"

"Nothing. Let's play."

Perry won 6-1, 6-0.

Back at the house Perry eagerly resumed his flirtation with the teenager. Peter went into the house to fetch two beers and when he returned to the back yard Perry and Lindsey were wrestling on the lawn.

Peter stared at them holding out the two beers in astonishment. Caitlin glared up at Peter from her lawn chair.

After dinner, he drove off to go call Jane. "Can I come over?"

"No."

"Why not?"

"Must there be a reason?"

"Yes of course, there's a reason for everything."

"I have company."

"There you go...a guy?"

"Yes."

"Okay then."

There was a pause then she said: "I'll talk to you later, okay?"

"Yeah, okay, sure." He hung up.

This certainly was not Peter's day. Two women whom he thought liked him now acted as if they couldn't care less if he dropped dead.

He drove to the Alki Tavern to drown his sorrows.

He arrived home at midnight. He tiptoed into the bedroom hoping not to wake Caitlin, and noticed something curious: Caitlin was not in bed. He turned on the light, and saw all the drawers were open and Caitlin's clothes were gone. He looked in the closet and they were gone from there too.

He looked into the bedrooms and the boys and Lindsey were gone. He carried on into the kitchen, wondering what was going on. His hands on his hips, he looked around the too quiet house and pondered the mystery of the missing bodies. He opened a beer and sat down at the kitchen table. There was a note on the table. He picked it up.

"Peter,

"I've been thinking of doing this for some time. Lindsey's step-father has left her mother so she's moving back home. The boys and I are staying with mom and dad until you and I can work things out or separate for good. I didn't want to do it this way, but I was afraid to confront you openly and have you talking me out of it. Your womanizing has become more than I can bear. I never thought I would hear myself saying this, but I don't think I love you anymore. How can you expect me to? I refuse to spend my life worrying while you're out catting around. I have to start living my life free of your insecurities and narcissistic trysts. Please don't call mom and dad's because they won't let you talk to me anyway. Cait."

He read it over again. He opened another beer. Was she serious?

He decided to go to bed and sleep on it. He was exhausted. He fell asleep immediately, but an hour later his heart went THUMP and he sat up sweating, his heart racing. He tossed and turned. He tried to read, but couldn't concentrate, He was reading a sensational new novel by the Czechoslovakian author Milan Kundera called *The Unbearable Lightness of Being*. Nothing had affected him like this novel in years. It was the novel he was trying to write. It would have immense influence on his own novel. It had romance, sexual intrigue, the unconscionable occupation of one country by another; all themes he was trying to incorporate into his novel about Vietnam. He read until daylight and then fell into a troubled sleep.

In the morning he fixed coffee and went to his study. He started typing, resuming his work on his Nam novel. He had decided to title his novel *Oldone*. He pulled up his Remington, and typed feverishly, pouring cup after cup of black coffee:

TWO

He stared at her. What should he tell her? About crawling through swamps while weird fungi attached themselves to him and began to eat away? About rats the size of cats and insects the size of rats? About death? About the time he was the only one back from an expedition and receiving the Silver Star for it—for surviving is all—when others were rewarded nothing for dying, not even a reason for their sacrifice? About the time he had a gook on his knees begging for his life and it never occurred to him not to kill him? About feeling no remorse, or pride, or anything other than the sheer horror of it all? Life became for him no longer a mystery to behold in fascination, but a nightmare to endure. Coming home with an empty feeling, a blank face for family and friends, incapable of explaining. His father was proud of him. A marine. A hero. Oldone didn't feel like a hero; he didn't feel like anything, hardly human. And now, belatedly, he feels fear, and he doesn't know of what. He jumps every time there's a loud noise. His nerves are frazzled. It's a joke at work. Knowing how he jumps, they sneak up behind him and drop flanges on the cement. And he shakes. The shakes stop when he drinks, and of course he drinks too much, though much less than when he first came home. He awakens in the middle of the night in a sweat thinking that he is still there. The drinking only delays the dreams; they build up in his subconscious waiting for a sober night then hit him spitefully all at once in one climactic nightmare.

Only after he'd come home did it occur to him to question why he'd gone. Only then did he consider the politics of it.

Trekking through the jungle, buddies all around him dropped like sick flies. But not him. Hardly a scratch. It was bizarre. He waited accordingly to be hit, and it never happened. He almost <u>wanted</u> it to happen; then he could go home. It gave him faith in fate. Providence, fairy god-mothers, whatever…There were too many close calls to not believe that someone was watching out for him.

Though his kind of fate happened to be mischievous—full of pranks.

He'd been drafted into the marines. Sitting in a large hall full of naïve 18 to 20 year olds about to go serve their country, a tall lean sergeant said, "We're going to be inducting one or two of you into the marines."

Oldone figured he would be among the one or two; at his young age he had already become aware of his kind of luck. He didn't gamble because he had soon discovered that he always lost. He had become convinced that it was a game providence played on him, having fun with him while chaperoning him. Games played as a boy: climbing trees, branches would break off and he would fall twenty feet into a blackberry patch, breaking his fall mercifully, but leaving him stricken with a body full of annoying scratches; thrown rocks from rowdy neighborhood bullies would whiz by each side of his head; greasy fifties teenagers in hopped up roadsters like Rebel Without a Causes careening around corners swerving enough to just miss him as he stood dreamily picking his nose.

Those going into the marines were to be called last. Oldone sat stoically in the huge hall packed with Baby Boomers each jumping up to be sworn into the army, sighing with relief at having escaped the dreaded marines. A lottery nobody won.

Except one. A pimply boy with bright red hair sat next to Oldone saying: "They ain't putting <u>me</u> in the marines, no way." He'd shake his head and sweat.

Eventually it was just Oldone and the boy sitting side by side in the hall, every sound a cold echo against the drab green emptiness. Oldone was calm, having already resigned himself to his fate.

But the boy beside him sat panicked despite his proclamation that he wasn't going. "I ain't goin'," he kept repeating until Oldone finally said, "I <u>believe</u> you, man." He didn't look even 18; freckles blending with the ripe pimples and no whiskers, he looked in the thick of confused adolescence.

"Charles Baldwin," the tall sergeant called out, and the young man sprang to attention, approaching the sergeant cautiously as if the sergeant was a dangerous animal.

The sergeant read off a clipboard. It was the first of many clipboards Oldone would be following around for two years. The sergeant must have been a slow reader; time crawled by silently. Baldwin stood at attention as if he was already sworn in. "It seems you have a criminal record."

"A criminal record?" Baldwin said.

"Did I stutter? You're on probation for car theft."

"Oh," Charles said, enlightened. "That."

"That," the sergeant mimicked. "You're being issued a waiver while the induction board reviews your record."

"A waiver?"

The sergeant drew an annoyed breath. "It <u>means</u> you have to go home... for now."

Charles Baldwin turned to Oldone with a victorious smile as if to say: "See?" He marched to the exit.

"Richard Old—un," the sergeant mispronounced, staring at the young recruit with the disgusting hippie beard and wild unkempt hair that was part gray despite his mere 18 years. "Guess where you're going." The sergeant smiled.

Eighteen year olds generally don't understand war. At least most 18 year olds didn't seem to understand this war. I didn't understand it, and in my confusion concluded that I couldn't be part of something I didn't understand. While Oldone was in the service I spent the time dodging the draft through various draft dodging schemes, finally securing a 4-F by putting dried egg yolk in my urine sample during a physical exam, which indicated that I had excessive albumin in my urine—whatever that is.

Ours was a generation that had been fed a steady diet of John Wayne and Audie Murphy movies. It would be more than a decade before movies such as "The Deer Hunter" and "Platoon" would pry open a proud nation's stubborn consciousness. Most 18 year olds then were heading off to Nam with fond memories of "The Sands of Iwo Jima" and "Hell is for Heroes".

Oldone was no different.

He returned from Nam still stunned by it, still not understanding it.

His parents met him at SeaTac with proud tears, and from there took him to a welcome home steak dinner at an expensive restaurant downtown.

He and his father got drunk together for the first time, and at home his father said the three words Oldone would soon grow weary of hearing and never be able to answer: "How was it?" with a wide proud of son and country smile, gratified that Richard wasn't like Christopher his second born who took drugs and had stringy unwashed hair half way down to his ass and was living in Canada to avoid the draft.

Chris is still in Canada, having established his home there, a carpenter living in a log cabin built with his own hands, with a wife and son, happier—I'm sure—then anyone else in Oldone's typically dysfunctional family.

Oldone's father stared at his oldest son as if he was going to describe an adventurous raft trip or journeys to romantic exotic locales, as if the tour had been done for sport. His father had fought in World War II, had fought in Europe. Surely <u>he</u> understood. Or had he forgotten?

Oldone's 14 year old sister Maureen sat, bored. His uncle was there, guzzling scotch with Oldone's father.

Oldone's uncle had also been in World War II, in the South Seas. He and Oldone's father were in business together. They both came home from work every night and drank until they passed out. His uncle had been at Pearl Harbor on December 7th, 1941. Didn't <u>he</u> understand?

Oldone tried to recall for the inquisitive family. Should he tell them how they threw garbage at Saigon peasants begging for food and laughing at them fighting for it like scavenging pigeons?

Or about the villages they destroyed, killing everybody in sight, elderly, women, children? Everybody was assumed to be VC. Even then, he didn't particularly hate the Vietnamese the way everybody else seemed to, the way his father and uncle still hated the Japanese. "They should have nuked the entire country," his father used to say.

He opened his mouth to speak, but no words came. Instead, for the first and last time, he cried. He cried for the horror witnessed, and the horrors committed. He put his hands to his face and bawled like a baby for the first time since he was a child.

Craving warmth and sentiment, especially from his mother, everyone instead seemed embarrassed for him.

Only 14-year-old Maureen consoled him. She ran to him and hugged him and cried with him while tears seeped through the tall fingers spread in shame over his face.

Maureen understood.

He didn't work for a year after he got out. He stayed with his parents, stayed loaded on pot, let his hair grow long again, and drank. It wasn't long before he had to drink an entire fifth of whiskey in order to maintain the numbness to his consciousness that he required. With marijuana though, he became less tolerant, to the point where he couldn't stand it anymore. Marijuana only magnified the nightmarish memories. Booze numbed the memories and prevented the nightmares.

He enrolled in the community college and learned how to weld.

He got a job as a welder while taking machinist classes at night. He worked in a machine shop for a year and a half before hiring in at Andresen Steel as a welder, then taking on the forklift job.

He learned how to cope with his nightmares.

Now he's the only offspring who still communicates with his parents. His parents, specifically his father, disowned Chris the day he left for Canada and has refused to speak to him since.

Maureen began taking drugs and skipping school, became withdrawn and rebellious. She ran away at the age of sixteen with a man on a Harley and hasn't been heard from since. Valliant attempts to find her have been in vain.

His parents are always asking him when he's going to get married and carry on the Oldone name, ignoring the fact that Chris has already done so.

His dad is 63 now, looks 75, overweight with dangerously high cholesterol and high blood pressure and diabetes, still religiously smoking three packs of Camel straights daily, drinking himself to s stupor every night. It had been a joke when he and Chris were kids, the old man would pass out in his chair in front of the TV with a half empty glass in his hand. They would pry it loose and put it in the kitchen. The old man would grumble, moan, stumble into the kitchen, grab the glass then go back to his chair and fall asleep again with the drink clutched in his hand like a pacifier.

Oldone has no idea when or if he's going to get married, has nothing against the institution, it's just that he hasn't as yet met the woman with whom he's prepared to spend the rest of his life (or who is prepared to spend the rest of her life with him). It is the one dilemma in his life he at least feels is a logical one. What's the rush? He has seen too many unhappy lives as a result of marriages that hadn't worked out, including his parents, who keep separate bedrooms (blaming each other's snoring) and hardly speak to each other.

"It wasn't bad," Oldone says to Yvette. "I stayed loaded or laid most of the time."

She laughs and cradles her head into the palms of each hand, like a basket, elbows on the table like pillars, eyes twinkling warmly at this most recent lover as if she'd like to keep him awhile. "I like you," she declares sincerely, an open invitation to a potential future.

He returns the smile, but not the compliment. He sips the coffee. His headache recedes.

"You political?" she says.

He ponders the question a moment. "I usually vote Democrat."

She nods. "I used to be a Marxist," she confesses.

"Used to be?" The coffee is drained. He rises to pour himself another cup.

"I'm not much of anything anymore."

"You're a good lover," he suggests.

"That's important." She frowns, lights a cigarette, her third so far this morning. "Too bad we didn't make it to Chelan."

"It was an impulsive idea anyway." To say the least, he thinks.

"Yes," she agrees, laughing.

"Another time?"

"Promise?"

In the sobriety and clarity of morning he sees what she really looks like. She could be over forty. Her blonde hair needs a fresh tinting; gray is evident at the roots. The lines around her eyes and mouth aren't as sexy or savory as they were under the dim lights and influence of several Black Russians.

"Why not?" he says, which to him is not a promise but a question without an answer.

"Breakfast?" she asks.

He shakes his head. "Thanks, no, I have to go."

She writes down her phone number for him. He stuffs the paper into his wallet where it will be forgotten until the next time he cleans out his wallet, kisses her goodbye, says he will call and knows that he will not.

It has rained during the night. The summer morning streets are clean and slick after the washing and cooling. The air smells fresh. The sky is color coordinated with Oldone's hair, as gray and dull as unpolished stainless steel. But then—the sun slips through the parted curtains of a cloud, thin yellow bursts through exuberantly.

Getting laid always makes him feel refreshed. It represses hangovers; he becomes rejuvenated, ready for the world…

Peter yanked the last page out of the typewriter and then reread what he had just typed.

"Shit," he said. "It's all shit."

He ripped the chapter to shreds.

NINETEEN

Peter sat across from Dean Rosen who had been staring at Peter without speaking for what seemed like several minutes. It was disconcerting. Finally he said:

"You look like shit."

"Thank you."

"I know that rumpled-Don Johnson-just-got drunk-and-laid look is in style now, but it doesn't suit you one bit."

"I'm having trouble sleeping."

"I think you should see someone."

"I have an appointment with my doctor to see about getting some sleeping pills."

"No, I mean a therapist of some sort. I'm worried about you, Peter. Not showing up for your classes simply will not do."

"I'll work on that."

"There's talk."

"Talk?"

"What you do with your private life is your business, but schtupping students half your age could get you into trouble. You don't want a harassment suit."

"Ah." Peter nodded. "My wife has left me."

Dean Rosen sighed. "I'm sorry, Peter, I really am, but can you blame her?"

"No."

"Take a couple weeks off. Get some rest. I'll have someone fill in for you."

Peter stood to leave.

"And Peter."

"Mm?"

"See someone. Get help."

———

After two sessions with Doctor Edelman, the esteemed psychiatrist arrived at three diagnoses: "Bipolar, attention deficit disorder, and post traumatic stress disorder from your experiences in Vietnam."

When he left for Vietnam, he had told Doctor Edelman, he was engaged to a girl. And then it seemed no one cared about the war. No one saw the point in shedding blood for a pointless war. War had crept up on him out of the blue and now he was caught in it like a rat in a trap. And he was in love with a woman half way around the world who was seldom writing back to him.

Everyone was stoned. Everything seemed to stand still. They woke up still stoned. They walked around stoned to the gills. They went out on patrols stoned out of their gourds.

There were no cheering crowds like in World War II. Villagers peeked out of their hooch's terrified. Peter had nothing against them. What was he doing here?

There were pot shots from no one knew where. All around him soldiers dropped like flies. But not him. He remained unscathed, miraculously. How come? He decided that fate had something else in store for him. He would someday write a novel about the Vietnam experience. It would be the greatest anti-war novel since *All Quiet on the Western Front*.

"And how's that going?" Doctor Edelman said.

He admitted the unfinished novel sat on his desk in haphazard notes, written in longhand over and over in spiral notebooks, just one chapter typed out that even that he wasn't entirely happy with.

"You haven't come to terms with the war yet," Doctor Edelman brilliantly deduced with all those years of psychological training at his disposal.

He had felt obligated to stay in Vietnam to delineate all the brutality of war, and then perhaps he could make sense of it. But he could not. The vast, infinite mystery of war confounded him to this day, and he could not get it out of his head onto the written page.

Doctor Edelman nodded his head wisely.

He had to admit, those Vietnamese were resolute, unlike the Americans. They seemed determined to keep shooting at them regardless.

"Soon we were running away from them like frightened squirrels, raving like lunatics, scooting for cover like scared rats, crisscrossing the jungle, jumping over tree roots, scampering back to safety."

Doctor Edelman nodded and kept taking notes.

"All anyone could think about was the end of their tour. 'Short!' others would scream at me egotistically as they came towards the end of their year-long nightmare. To me it was an eternity away.

"And the system actually encouraged this? Shooting at people was not only okay, it was a mandate? Upstanding citizens passed laws that said I must kill people I had nothing against? I hadn't thought about it that way until now. There must be some mistake, I thought…

"I watched as a corporal pointed his pistol point blank at his own left boot and squeezed the trigger. He screamed…I screamed out for a medic. The corporal smiled at me, red trembling strips of skin and bone poking out from the end of his blown away boot. 'I get to go home,' he said to me, winking as if he had one over the world. 'Say hello to mom,' I said back.

"I took off my helmet and sat down on it, and only then realized I had shit my pants, the stench now creeping up into my nostrils as I had a smoke and watched the mindless medics put the laughing corporal on a stretcher and haul him away.

"It was then I realized that the war was over for me. I was done. 'What are you doing!' some sergeant said. 'Having a smoke.' 'Jesus Christ, you stink! Did you shit your pants?' 'Yes, sergeant.' 'Get the fuck back to your unit and get the fuck cleaned up.'

"It seemed there was nothing but flames, smoke, and noise. Bullets whizzed past my ears like buzzing bees. There seemed no rhyme or reason for it. It was all chaos and disorder. At night I couldn't sleep. I couldn't get the flames, smoke, and noise out of my head. I waited to die.

"Then the monsoons came and were endless. The jungle was a swamp. In addition to malaria, I'd picked up some kind of jungle rot."

This jungle rot was a foot fungus that eventually infected his toenails with a thick yellow crust. Over the years women on one night stands would say to him, "You always sleep with your socks on?"

He didn't tell Doctor Edelman this.

"And then naturally—not unexpectedly—came the 'Dear John' letter from Eva, which didn't help matters. Whatever ambition I had formerly was kaput completely. No brilliant novel was forthcoming in my thoughts anymore, not even a mediocre one. My daily mundane duties became tortuous tasks. Smoking dope didn't help, of course. Someone offered me heroin, but I had the fortitude to decline."

Time became distorted. Incidents that had happened just the day before were put deep into his subconscious. Hours became days. Days became months, months years. He became a recluse. Officers looked at him and shook their heads. A Chickenshit at heart, he became terrified of life.

He sat with the others and watched John Wayne in *The Green Berets*. While everyone laughed at this farcical piece of shit propaganda, all he could think about was Eva. *The fucking bitch. The stinking whore cunt. I'll get her!* "While I was over there keeping the world safe, she was fucking someone else."

Doctor Edelman kept nodding and jotting notes.

He would smoke a joint to forget her and only think about her more. The Saigon prostitutes couldn't even get him past half mast. "You like boys?" one said to him. "We can get you pretty boy. We have *beaucoup* pretty boys!"

It was absurd, why he continued to smoke dope when he didn't even like it, what it was doing to him. He hated dope and he hated cigarettes and he continued to smoke both like a masochist.

"There's another diagnosis for you, Doctor: masochist."

Doctor Edelman stopped writing and stared at him meditatively.

"I have a question for you, Doctor."

"All right. Go ahead."

"Who is the greatest poet in history?"

Doctor Edelman continued to stare at Peter with reflection. He answered: "That's sort of out of my expertise, Peter."

"I'll tell you who is the greatest poet in the English language, and that is John Keats."

"All right."

"Or Percy Shelley…Or Lord Byron. At any rate, the Romantics."

"I see." He nodded with feigned interest, and resumed writing.

"And who is the greatest novelist in history?" Peter enquired.

"Hemingway?" Doctor Edelman guessed.

"Dostoyevsky is."

"Ah." Edelman nodded his head agreeably.

"Or Tolstoy. Or Joyce. Or Fitzgerald. Or Faulkner. Or Hardy."

Edelman continued to stare at Peter as though he had a lunatic on his hands.

"But that's not who my students want to read. You know who my students want to read? These bright college students? These future leaders of our country? They are not interested in the poetry of John Keats or Percy Shelley; they want to read Charles Bukowski!"

"I don't know Charles Bukowski."

"And you're better off for it! He's a drunken, vulgar bum and a terrible writer! And they don't want to read Fyodor Dostoyevsky or Thomas Hardy; they want to read Kurt Vonnegut! An overrated science fiction hack!"

Doctor Edelman sighed, quickly glanced at his watch then hurried Peter out the door with a prescription for a mood stabilizer. And thinking that he could smell alcohol on him, he added: "Be sure to not drink alcohol," he warned.

"Right."

TWENTY

Perry had an addictive personality. After he got off methadone he became addicted to sugar, which made him fat, so he kicked sugar and became addicted to tennis, bicycling, and running, which at least were healthy addictions—he thought. He kicked his unhealthy addiction to Lynn by meeting Annette, whom he met at a tennis tournament, where he won the B division, she the A. He invited her out to hit, and they hit if off. They got married and had two children, a boy and a girl. He became a supervisor at an engineering firm in Bellevue, and she was a registered nurse at Virginia Mason Hospital. They bought a 2500-square foot home in Bellevue and were living the American Dream. He supplemented his addiction to exercise with a thirst quenching six-pack of beer every night.

Sometime around the mid-1990s, Perry began having abdominal pains and aching joints and his workouts weren't going well. These symptoms didn't alleviate, so he went to see his doctor. His doctor took blood tests and said he had hepatitis C. "What does that mean?" His doctor wasn't sure what it meant, and sent him to a liver specialist. The liver specialist said he would be dead in five years if he didn't get a liver transplant.

Paul Placik was famous—or was to become famous—as a furniture maker. Having learned everything his father and grandfather could teach him in regards to working with wood—he transcended even these monumental skills that had been passed down from many generations, even before electricity was even a glint in Benjamin Franklin's eyes.

He built a house with his own hands on Whidbey Island on five acres of dense Douglas fir and Western Red Cedar. He built the house without removing one live tree. Perry designed it. He told Perry that he didn't want any toxic chemicals in his house. There would be no carpets emitting toxic gases. He was "green" before that was an adjective meaning "environmentally conscientious." He would use a water based finish on bamboo floors. The cedar deck would go unfinished. The walls would have twelve inch thick insulation to keep the house warm in the winter without oil or electric heat, and cool during the summer without air conditioning. He would install a wood-burning stove in which he would feed the seasoned wood that had fallen on his property. There would be passive solar heating energy and expansive triple-paned windows facing mostly south. Perry would design, and Paul would build, a 500-gallon water cistern that collected rain water and would be recycled for watering, cleaning, and drinking; and a compostable toilet, having studied ancient Rome plumbing. "*Fuck* the utility companies!" Paul told Perry.

"There will have to be some toxins in at least the caulking," Perry said.

"There won't be any calking," Paul told him.

"There has to be at least *some* calking!" Perry argued.

"No, the joints will be so precise I won't need to calk," and indeed, Paul made the joints so precise that after he had applied primer and water based paint no one could tell that he had not calked.

Paul married a beautiful Asian woman named Rosalie. They had three daughters in quick yearly succession like prompt appointments. Paul's huge muscular body that was so feared on the soccer field got even bigger, mostly in his belly. On their regular hikes in the Cascades and Olympics with his two older brothers he could no longer keep up. They yelled at him to step it up. He yelled back: "I got three kids!" "What the fuck that got to do with the price of pot in Poulsbo!" Perry yelled back. "Get your fat ass in gear, goober gut!"

Paul had to quit playing soccer. His poor aching knees could no longer withstand the pressure of his 260 pounds.

As for Peter, he was back with Caitlin and being a good boy—for now. He kept referring to the "Nam novel" he was writing. But no one was taking him seriously anymore, not even his literary agent who gave up asking about it. And yet again Jackson needed a place to crash.

TWENTY-ONE

Consciousness came to Jackson in rapid, uncertain sequences. One moment he was a young man seducing a pretty woman in his newly bought home, in the next the woman had disappeared before the seduction could manifest itself, but he was still young: handsome, muscular, witty as ever, enterprising as an entrepreneur, energetic, in the midst of his indefatigable twenties. This fantasy prevailed as he pried open eyelids practically sealed shut from dried mucus and was presented with a piss yellow world. Lingering in this twilight land of murky awareness, it slowly dawned on Jackson despairingly that he was not a young man in his twenties, but in fact forty—and no longer handsome or muscular.

Pushing himself laboriously to a sitting position he looked around this room that appeared mysteriously bare and realized that he had spent the night on the living room floor in his own house—or that is—his foreclosed house.

Hoge was curled up in the fetal position on the sofa, hands between his thighs, chest heaving and throat snorting in aching, desperate ingestions of oxygen. Last night came to Jackson, hazy, but no dream.

Hoge and he had been busy packing, ironically united in an enterprise that had responsibility and purpose. They were all smoked up and almost enjoying themselves just like the old days. But like most jobs throughout their collaborative lives, this one too was cut short when inevitably, Hoge disappeared without notice, reappearing hours later with a half empty bottle of McNaughton's and a wrinkled Lotto ticket, the latter of which he dropped on the coffee table dismissively, mumbling some nonsense about winning.

Instinctively, Jackson had rushed to the kitchen for two glasses with ice, returning to the living room to pour the whiskey, politely handing Hoge his, only to find Hoge passed out on the sofa. So he drank both glasses, and continued to refill his glass with whiskey and ice until the bottle was empty, and he curled up on his well-worn carpet content with his happy drunk dreams.

So yet again they were in a predicament of having to rush. He gently nudged his old friend with his left foot. "Come on, Hoge, we've got to move it."

No response whatsoever.

Friends since high school, Hoge was the creative one. In art class, his talent was so blatant he was insulting to his teachers. Even with his precocious doodles with pencil or charcoal, one could see that here was an individual whose art transcended mere talent. While Hoge's genius was what he put on canvas, Jackson's was in his innate charm. And they both survived on these talents for many years. Life on the fringes can be construed as a romantic sign of rebellion in youth, but in middle age it becomes sad and humiliating, further compromised by the loss of sexy good looks that comes with age and dissipation.

And as irresponsible as Jackson had been over the years, he was the epitome of reliability and stability compared to Hoge. He'd been carrying Hoge for over twenty years now, through each of their tumultuous marriages, rescuing him from one scrape after another. And while Jackson was the one with the charm and silver tongue even when stumbling drunk, Hoge was always an obnoxious drunk. He'd start fights and invariably get beat up. Though he stood a solid six-foot and weighed a sturdy 200, he couldn't fight a lick. When sober, no one was more aware of this innate handicap than he was. But when drunk he seemed to think of himself gifted with the pugilistic skills of a Mohammed Ali or Sonny Liston. Jackson had rescued him from manslaughter time after time, his magic tongue going a mile a minute as he yet again pulled a cursing and belligerent Hoge away from certain massacre.

As the reader knows by now, Jackson could talk people right out of their pants, if Jackson wanted them to think he was in dire need of a pair. This gift of rhetoric—grandiloquent yet subservient—had held onto the house this long, with promises of forthcoming payments. He had the uncanny ability to make people believe his promises were bona fide despite his infamous history. And he *was* sincere, that was the irony. He never intended to not pay his bills. But this particular onus of responsibility evaded Jackson like a million dollar lottery. Even when he had the money in the bank (which was a challenging enough manifestation in itself), he simply was incapable of completing the sequence of sitting down at the kitchen table, writing out the check, putting the signed check into an envelope, sealing the envelope, putting a stamp on the envelope, and toting it dutifully up to the corner mailbox. Always somewhere along this natural order of protocol that most of us follow as simply as A-B-C, he would never arrive at his prescribed destination: the corner mailbox. Oftentimes he would get so far as to write the check and seal the envelope. But more times than not, he wouldn't have the stamps, and even when he did, the house payment or city light payment or whatever would shuffle around on the kitchen table until long forgotten or misplaced, and naturally by then there wouldn't be the money in the bank to cover the check anyway. The only way Jackson had ever been able to pay a bill is if a creditor happened to come along on the odd occasion when Jackson happened to have cash on his person or money in his account, when then of course Jackson would be more than happy to pay up, with interest.

He shuffled to the bathroom, bloated bladder about to burst. He stood anxiously over the toilet, feeling as if he would be purged internally in a rupture of toxicity if his bladder did not immediately cooperate. And not untypically, it did not. It was as if there existed a thin yet tenacious membrane between bladder and urethra. He tried the usual remedies: turning on the faucet and staring hypnotically at the flow; closing his eyes and counting backwards from one hundred. Neither worked. "*Please*, God! I'm dying here!" He trembled, cold sweat dotted his wrinkled, stress-etched brow…At last… the faithless little one-eyed dipstick erupted with an avalanche of copper colored poisons. "Oh God, thank you so much, I'll go and never sin again," he whimpered submissively—another sincere promise destined for failure— right thumb and forefinger guiding the violent flow in a tremble, his left palm flush against the cracked dry-rotting back wall balancing himself bent-kneed. Two minutes later he was still squeezing long-lingered waste out in sequential spurts from the agonizing push of his pitiful prostate.

Back in the living room, he kicked Hoge again, harder this time.

Hoge stirred, pushed himself up on one arm, smacked his parched lips, stared pensively across the worn, lint-etched carpet, then collapsed back down.

Jackson stood hands on hips like a foreman. Open cardboard boxes still filled the calamitous abode. Drawers angled open; cupboard doors spread like wings. He squinted outside at the quiet gray atmosphere, up the long driveway to where his old '65 Chevrolet ¾ ton pickup resided, rusting at the crest since its starter motor was too unpredictable to leave at the foot of the hill by the front walk. It had been a beautiful late summer's day yesterday, but now it was raining, a silent mist soaked into mattresses and sofa, rusting bed springs. "Shit."

Hoge stumbled directly to the bathroom to quickly relieve himself. Hoge did not suffer the same kidney issues of his best friend. Incredibly, despite his self-abuse, *everything* worked on Hoge. He even masturbated regularly, an inclination Jackson seldom had these days. Hoge even looked good, erect and handsome; his thick coils of graying hair the only clue to his forty-one years.

From bathroom directly to the refrigerator he trekked only to discover that which he had to know was fact but apparently needed confirmation: there was no beer. He stared for a dejected moment, then collapsed in a kitchen chair and stared morosely across the cracked linoleum.

"We gotta go, Hoge."

Reminded of this, Hoge peaked at the eviction notice still unfolded conspicuously on the kitchen table, reading it over quickly as if that still required personal confirmation as well, as if perhaps there had been some kind of mistake.

Jackson busily hauled full boxes out to the pickup. Hoge stood and emptied a glass of water down his throat in vociferous gulps, water trickling down each side of his white whiskered cheeks.

They were ready to go. Hoge was in the passenger side of the pickup, head angling against the window, eyes closed.

Jackson looked around at the house that had been his for several years, happened to glance down at the coffee table they were leaving behind and spotted Hoge's Lotto ticket. He picked it up, a $5 ticket, and noticed that one line had all six numbers circled. He stared at it a moment, wondered if perhaps it really was a winning ticket, a multi-million dollar winning ticket, chuckled ironically at this absurd thought, but stuck the wrinkled piece of paper in his wallet anyway, just in case.

TWENTY-TWO

Jackson was over at Peter and Caitlin's. He was ignoring Dusty, their golden retriever, who was siding up to him, seeking attention. Caitlin was busy washing the inside of the living room window, trying to ignore her brother.

"Want me to do the outside?"

She scrubbed harder with the paper towel. She didn't answer.

"What's wrong?"

She stopped wiping, stepped back and looked for smears, stepped forward, wiped some more with a critical eye.

"Cait?"

His list of people to go to had dwindled away. He had disappointed too many too many times so that even his innate charm was losing ground. Even their parents had given up on him and had refused to enable him further. He knew only in soft-hearted Caitlin had he a smidgen of a chance.

She sighed as if suddenly exhausted by her labor, collapsed on the sofa across from him head bouncing playfully against the back of the sofa, legs spread. Dusty rubbed against her. She scratched his back.

"Where's your pickup?"

"It's broke down over at Hoge's mother's house, where I left him."

"She's taken him in?"

"For awhile."

"Brave woman." She looked back at the results of her labor, and out, across Alki Beach to the city, clear from a recent rain, to the Cascades, capped with dwindling snow. She seemed lost in thought, as if she'd forgotten all about him.

135

"I know you can use some help around here."

"Where's Peter's mountain bike, Jacky?"

He looked away guiltily, following her gaze to Alki Beach.

She glared at him. "Where's the hundred bucks you borrowed last time you were over?"

"I'll pay you back."

"You'll *what?* Don't bullshit me, Jacky."

He threw up his hands in surrender. "Okay. You're right." He stood.

"It has nothing to do with right or wrong. It's a matter of self-respect. A person can take only so much before losing all sense of dignity."

He shuffled across the hard wood floor, head dangling.

"When are you going to grow up, Jacky?"

He shrugged, like a reprimanded ten-year-old.

"Sooner or later everyone has to accept responsibility for their actions."

"I know."

"You're not eighteen anymore."

He nodded.

"You're lucky to be alive."

"No, I'm not. I'd be better off dead."

"You can skip the melodrama."

Dusty stood with Jackson at the door, not about to miss any opportunity for escape.

They paused staring at each other like reluctant lovers splitting up. Three years younger than he, she was still beautiful. All the stress that Peter and he had put on her hadn't affected her looks. Peter and Caitlin were still a great looking couple, the best looking of all of them. Her thick hair still had its strawberry sheen, her pale freckled face smooth and unlined as a twenty year old, her figure as lean as it was before the boys were born.

"Okay," she said, relenting as usual.

She was well aware that she was enabling him, but couldn't seem to help it. The thought of her brother out on the streets homeless and vulnerable to the elements was too much to bear. "But this is the last time." How many times had she said that? She'd lost count, as he had lost count of how many DUI's he'd accumulated over the years.

"I won't disappoint you, Cait." How many times had he said those words? "I'll help out around here."

"I know you will. You always do. That's not the point, and you know it."

"I know."

"You know the rules."

He nodded wholeheartedly. "Don't worry."

"Right. And I still have to talk to Peter."

He nodded, knowing he didn't have to worry about that: Peter was a softer touch than his sister.

"And when you're not helping out around here, I don't want you sitting around watching the Mariners. I expect something productive out of you." For some reason, that drove her crazy, his sitting for hours in front of the TV.

He nodded agreeably, as always.

"And another thing, when you empty the ice tray, fill it up with water and put it back in the freezer—that drives Peter nuts when he doesn't have any ice."

———

Jackson sat on the back deck with a glass of ice water, having a smoke, tossing a tennis ball out on the lawn for Dusty to retrieve. It was warm, but that wouldn't last long; he could already feel the slight chill of encroaching autumn.

Everything hurt: his gut, his joints, his head; even his asshole hurt. He could feel what he assumed was an enlarged liver pressing against his lower right rib cage, tight and bloated. Last time he saw a doctor he was told his next drink could be his last. Lot he knew.

He flicked his cigarette out to the vegetable garden, Dusty following the trajectory with a keen interest, wondering if he was supposed to retrieve it. He and Dusty stepped inside. The dog flopped down with a resigned grunt, panting and staring at Jackson stupidly. Jackson ambled to the fridge, hungry, or what he assumed to be hunger, this annoying, bloated nausea he had in his gut.

The fridge was high and tight with food, as if anticipating Armageddon. He knew that this was an issue with Peter, Caitlin coming home from Costco with boxes stuffed with provisions, most of which they would never consume, huge jars of mayonnaise and peanut butter that would eventually go bad, throw-away plastic razors littering the house, piles of toilet paper stacked in the basement. We all had our little phobias.

His hunger dissipated in an instant as he spotted a specific item stuffed into a door shelf: a can of Budweiser. Surprised that it was there, since Caitlin discouraged alcohol in the house these days, Peter on a sabbatical from drinking as well since he was on some kind of medication, but without further meditation on its origins, he pulled it out like a plug and snapped it open, draining it in seconds.

He shut the door quickly wondering where to hide the evidence and turned to face, of course, Caitlin.

"If I don't quit gradually, I'll go through withdrawals."

She nodded arms crossed, as if sympathetic. "Then you'll have to withdraw somewhere else."

"Cait…"

"You couldn't stick to the rules even ten minutes! That's it! Get out! I've had it! You'll never stop drinking! Never! Not until you've killed yourself! Go kill yourself somewhere else! I won't watch you do it!"

There was no point in arguing when she was like this with that unpredictable Irish temper of hers. He grabbed his coat, and left.

TWENTY-THREE

Peter was playing tennis at the Alki courts and thought he recognized her at least one hundred feet away on the soccer field, tall and lean as always, her five-foot-ten a head above the crowd of women on the field. The old feelings of anxiety were returning, fogging his head. He hadn't seen her since before he left for Vietnam. He felt himself coming apart in the dusty gray heat, his memory like a wrinkled old black-and-white photograph.

When he finished his match he carried his racket and gear down the grassy knoll to confirm it. She had seen him too, had recognized him too, and they came timidly towards each other.

"It's been a long time," he said.

"Twenty years? Maybe longer."

"You look great."

"You too."

The coach was calling out to her impatiently.

"I have to get back. The second half is starting."

He sat down on the bench and watched the second half—why, he didn't know. Her height was in her long lean legs, and she used them well: she was fast, coordinated, and aggressive. She scored a goal, and their team won the game.

Afterwards she plopped down next to him with a satisfied sigh.

"You're a good player."

She laughed. "You need to come to my games more often. 'Eva! What's happened to you!' the coach said about my sudden aggressiveness and hustle."

"You're fast."

"Yes, I am!" she said, as if the fact surprised even herself.

"I didn't know you were an athlete."

"I wasn't twenty years ago."

"Who was?"

"I remember you as an athlete. Don't think I wasn't checking you out on the tennis court. You hit well."

"Do you play tennis?"

"Not like you."

"That's okay. We'll have to hit."

She regarded him suspiciously. "Are you still married to Caitlin?"

"Yes. Are you still married to Mathew?"

"Oh no! That ended ages ago!"

He had heard, but he didn't want her to know that he knew.

"I'm surprised," he said. "You really don't look any different." This was true, yet somehow she looked the age that she was.

"I'm 38," she said.

"I can count."

They laughed.

He felt a sudden flush of blood to his head. He felt nausea and anger. He wanted to hit her. He wanted to fuck her. The field was silent and empty. They walked up to the street where her car was parked, the warm summer evening graying with dwindling light, arms crossed, deep in conversation. She always had been a talker.

"I hear you're a college professor," she said.

"Yes," he said, shrugging dismissively.

"What do you teach?"

"English Lit."

"That's exciting. We'll have to talk more."

Now it was he who looked at her with some doubt.

"It's not that exciting. And you?"

"I'm working as a Teacher's Aid right now. I got a degree in Economics, then decided to get a degree in history. I can't make up my mind. I'm what is derogatively referred to as a 'professional student'. I'm working on my Ph.D. in Linguistics. I've always been interested in it."

"Do you like Chomsky?"

"I love Chomsky. I studied under him one quarter."

He smiled at her appreciatively.

She laughed. "I hear you write as well."

"I scribble a bit."

"Actually, I read your book of short stories. You're more than a scribbler."

"You bought my book? You were the one?"

She laughed. "I've thought a lot about you over the years, Peter."

He ignored this, and said, "I'm working on a novel about Vietnam."

"Of course you are."

He looked at her. She went on talking about how she had travelled extensively. She spoke Italian, French, Portuguese, and Spanish. "They all kind of run together."

"Yes, the romance languages. I can speak a little Spanish and can manage my way ordering lunch at a French café."

"Can you read French and Spanish?"

"*Naturellement*. I read *L'Etranger*."

"How about Sartre?"

"He's too ponderous in English."

She laughed. "What do you think of these experimental writers who are so popular now? Barth? Pynchon? Barthelme?"

"I prefer the realistic fiction of Cheever, Carver, and Beatty. But that's just me."

"I'm the same." She nodded enthusiastically. She studied him. "You look different," she said, taking him in from head to toe. "But you sure look good." She smiled coyly.

"Obviously we both stay in shape."

"I still smoke a little pot now and again," she admitted.

"I smoked enough back then to last a lifetime."

"You didn't smoke that much."

"You weren't there." He said this as accusation, and she seemed suddenly embarrassed.

They were standing next to a beat-up Volkswagen Bug, her car. It was interesting; it looked almost exactly like the car he had when they were dating. He wondered if that meant anything.

"Let's get together for coffee...or a drink," he added.

She stared uncertainly. "I think I would like that. We'll catch up."

Peter had a bad habit of showing up for engagements unfashionably early. But Caitlin was the exact opposite, so they usually balanced each other out time wise. Right now he had nervously quaffed two White Russians waiting. Eva arrived fifteen minutes late, at 8:15.

She apologized for being late.

"It's okay. I was just enjoying a drink by myself. In fact, I was enjoying it so much I'd appreciate it if you would go someplace else to sit."

She laughed. "I see your sense of humor hasn't changed."

Dry as the bone I have for you, he thought within his slight buzz.

They ordered drinks.

"This is my first alcohol in over a year," he said.

"Oh?"

"I'm on medication. Not supposed to drink."

"Are you all right?"

"Yes, just a mood stabilizer. I was having issues with my temper and concentration and went to a shrink."

"Anything to do with Vietnam?"

"As a matter of fact. But also, it seems I have ADD and am bipolar."

"So, who doesn't? Who isn't?"

He laughed. "It's what the shrink said, I dunno. The ADD is why I could never get past page one hundred of *Atlas Shrugged*."

She laughed.

"And Perry and Paul always humiliated me in chess. Seriously, it was hard to get past my math requirements for college. And he thinks I have a milder form of bipolar or manic depression, which explains my mood swings. Therefore, the mood stabilizers. But I don't see any difference. So fuck it, I haven't been taking the meds the last few days, so I'll drink instead. It helps best."

She laughed. "I want to read your novel."

"When it's ready."

"How long have you been working on it?"

"Don't ask."

"How long have you been working on it?"

They laughed. It came back to him now in a rush, how much they laughed. They decided it was too noisy there, so after finishing their drinks they went to a quieter bar and sat in a secluded corner. The ambience was soft. The music was low and jazzy. The waitress flirted with Peter, and Peter said: "She's angling for a tip."

Eva regarded him doubtfully. "You're gorgeous, and you know it."

They started snuggling and kissing. Then she violently pushed him away. "Whoa! What are we doing!"

"Getting reacquainted."

"Peter! Do you have *affairs?*"

"I haven't for some time."

"I'm disappointed."

"Did you think I was a good little boy all these years?"

"Actually, I had this fantasy that you were. I envisioned you to be this perfect husband and father living the perfect middle-class life and all the comforts that go with it." She, on the other hand, told him she had nothing: no husband, no kids, no home ownership—just a series of horror story relationships.

"On the other hand you have your freedom, your friends, your traveling." She shrugged. "So?"

"You're not seeing anyone right now?"

"Really, Peter, there's not much out there. There are a whole slew of alcoholics, drug addicts, derelicts, unemployables, rednecks, beer-bellied ignoramuses who sit around watching football, assholes, and sickos."

"You're too picky."

She laughed uproariously. "And married men," she added.

She admitted she went to bars to meet men. She got lonely and didn't know where else to go. So she found company for a night. "I could tell you stories."

"Searching for Mr. Goodbar?"

"Yes."

He didn't like thinking of Eva into this lifestyle and was surprised she admitted to it. For some reason, he expected her to be the innocent girl he had de-virginized. There was the bipolar little boy of him that had expected her to have remained faithful to him these last twenty years.

And she had expected him to be a faithful, dutiful husband.

"Are we going to have an affair?" she said.

"Yes," he said, assertively. "*Naturellement.*"

She lifted her glass. "*Salut!*"

They resumed their hugging and kissing. "I can't believe how comfortable I feel with you."

It was his downfall, this comfort women felt.

They were instantly attracted to each other, as they had been twenty years before when they had been fumbling, bumbling, just out of adolescence, stoned to the gills hippies. But they were middle-aged adults now, established in their lives, immersed in their prime, journeypersons.

"You have a good body," she said, running her hands over it "I'm glad you take care of yourself. So many men don't bother."

"I drink too much."

She shrugged that off. "One must have some vices."

"You have a good body too."

"I make it a priority. I do one hour of yoga every morning; then I meditate."

"Ommm." They laughed.

He followed her home. Eva lived in one of those grand old structures in the University District that was shared by students. She shared the house with three others. The old cedar shakes were tilting and rotting. The roof was thick with moss. The wood gutters were rotting and not functioning. Rain poured off the sides of the house. Eva had a room.

After they had made love twice, she said: "I'd forgotten how potent you are."

"It's a gift."

"Humble too, I see."

They laughed and laughed.

"You'd come and stay hard as a rock. I've never known another guy like that."

"I was twenty."

"Yes. My poor coodie!"

"Coodie?"

"It's what my sister and I have always called it."

They laughed and laughed.

"Are you secure in other parts of your life?" she said, serious.

"I have doubts."

"Such as?"

144

"I've always had doubts of my intelligence. I struggled in school. But I was determined to finish."

"And you've done extremely well."

"And it turns out it has nothing to do with intelligence. When it comes to logic my brain comes to a dead end. All that left brain stuff eluded me."

"You're the creative type."

"Yeah…well…There's a narcissistic part of me that expects no less than ultimate recognition of my innate genius while another part of me wonders if I have any talent at all…It's all very complicated in all that Freudian Oedipal shit."

"You have issues with your mother?"

"I did *not* have sex with my mother."

They laughed.

"I have issues with both my parents. But my mother wasn't there, emotionally. She carried bitterness against my father. She's from Australia and they met during the war. She wishes now she had never left."

"Why doesn't she return?"

"She says because of us, her sons."

"She does love you then."

Peter shrugged. They lay naked on her brass antique bed. She was mindlessly playing with him again, making him hard again.

"Could there be something there in how you treat women?"

He turned his head towards her in shock and dismay, as if it were an insight never uncovered. His therapist certainly hadn't.

"Forget I said that."

She continued to use his cock as a play thing, observing its magic.

"I spent one night with a guy whose cock was as thick as your wrist and as long as your forearm."

"Changing the subject, are we?"

They laughed and laughed.

———

At the cabin in Chelan she looked around at family pictures and became depressed. He was discovering that she became depressed easily. *Maybe I should give her my mood stabilizers,* he mused…Her ever changing moods were beginning to wear on him. In some ways she was as fragile as swallows' eggs, in other ways as hard and unbending as steel. She was as temperamental as the teenager he had known so well, as if she was reverting to that time. She made *him* depressed with her moods. They quarreled like long-term lovers, as if their relationship was progressive, like an alcoholic who takes up drinking after a long sabbatical from it. It was silly.

She refused to have sex with him. Except in the morning she had him go down on her. She twisted convulsively, as if caught in a painful spasm. Her taste was exquisite. When he moved towards here, she said: "No!"

"Why not?"

"I've got a lot getting even to do," she said ironically and inexplicably.

The weekend in Chelan they had been looking forward to with such heightened anticipation like children on Christmas Eve had turned out disastrously. All because of a few silly pictures.

On their way home she didn't speak. She looked out at waterfalls and formations of rock eons old, formed after the last ice age had melted. She spoke at last: "I wish I knew more about geology."

"You could always get another degree," he replied churlishly.

She looked at him sadly, warmly. She was no longer angry. *What the fuck?* he wondered. Abra cadabra, she gave him a blow job going over Snoqualmie Pass.

She alternated between depression and gaiety, fun and seriousness in triggered instants. He never knew what to expect of her, or when to expect it. She kept saying that their relationship was doomed, yet she kept seeing him. He decided they were too much alike.

She told him about Mathew. He had been jealous of Peter and always wanted her to compare Peter to him as lovers. She didn't dare say he was anything but the best. He was possessive and jealous. Shortly after they married he began beating her. She put up with it because she was naïve and liberal, and thought she could change him. He was dyslexic, and it had gone undiagnosed. It was because of Mathew she developed an interest in linguistics. He was a functional illiterate who could barely read. She tried to teach him. He didn't have the patience, and would go into rages. She came home from school one day, and he had torn up all her school work. It littered the floor. He was sitting on the floor in the midst of the rubble crying like a child. He wailed that he was

sorry. She tried consoling him, saying it was okay, knowing that it was dangerous to get angry with him, that he would beat her. Then he beat her anyway,
worse than ever. She had broken ribs, a broken jaw, smashed nose, bloody and
purple eyes. She drove herself to the hospital. She couldn't tell her parents
because she didn't want her strict Southern Baptist mother to know that she
had married a wife beater. She tried to get in touch with Peter, but discovered
that he was married to Caitlin.

Peter was shocked. He had been a friend of Mathew. He had admired him,
with his James Dean looks and expertise behind the wheel of whatever junker
he was working on at the time. Mathew laughed like a madman as he down-
shifted and played with the clutch, accelerator, and brakes and maneuvered
around objects with athletic like precision. Peter had always felt safe with him
regardless of how recklessly he drove.

"What did you do?"

"I went over there one day when he wasn't there, grabbed my stuff, and
left. I never saw him again. He never showed up in court for the divorce. He
married Susan Banyon, and their baby died."

"I remember that incident. It was an accident, they said."

"That's what they said, but I don't believe it. I think he killed his baby. He
was insane. He was a coward and a bully. He was contemptible"

"Did he do a lot of drugs?"

"He couldn't handle drugs. They made him even more insane. Alcohol too.
He avoided them."

He was the first of a series of bad experiences with men. "I realized then I
had let the best of them get away."

"And as you have discovered, I am no saint."

"Oh, I wasn't talking about you."

He looked at her. They laughed and laughed.

———

They went to foreign films and tried not to read the subtitles. They browsed
through bookstores. They sat in espresso bars and read quietly. They played
tennis. They went running. They got down on the carpet and pounded out
pushups, laughing hysterically. They were both tall, lean, and quick. They were

manic and happy when they were like this. When they drank they got depressed and argued.

She had two sets of friends. She had her intellectual friends at the university, and she had her redneck cohorts in West Seattle. She alternated between them in antithetic loyalty, from the University District to West Seattle like Jekyll and Hyde, from brains in school to debauchery at the Alki Tavern, from one schizophrenic entity to another.

———

"How's Jackson?" she said one day.

"Drinking himself into an early grave."

"Hm."

———

Caitlin stayed awake each night watching TV until he got home. Sometimes he didn't get home. She didn't sleep. She was exhausted by him. She didn't know what to do. She had thought he had outgrown it. She had been wrong.

Eva became more demanding of his time, needing to see him when he couldn't. Whenever he couldn't see her she became depressed and angry.

Caitlin demanded he give her up, whoever she was.

Eva's roommate and best friend Ann seemed distant and aloof to him. She didn't seem to like him. He was not used to this. Everyone liked him. His students adored him. He was a nice guy to a fault.

"Ann doesn't seem to like me."

"She doesn't know you. She knows me, and she worries about me because I keep seeing men who are no good for me."

He said something stupid: "You aren't the first woman in the world to have an affair with a married man."

Her face twisted to its familiar ominous scowl and she said: "It's called solidarity, Peter. I am betraying my sex. I am betraying Caitlin."

———

Peter and Eva were the latest scandal in West Seattle. Caitlin knew. She told him she knew.

"What are you going to do?" he said.

"I called her. We're going to meet."

Caitlin got into bed with Peter after being with Eva all night. She made sure he was awake. Eva had tried to defend her behavior to Caitlin. She said she was in love with Peter and couldn't stay away from him. She had tried to, but couldn't.

"Shame on you," Caitlin said to Peter. "You're mean and cruel. You're deceitful and thoughtless. How could you do that to that poor girl?"

"You know what she said to me?"

"What, Peter? What did she say to you?"

"She said she had fucked other men while I was in Vietnam."

"And I supposed you were true blue while you were away."

"Touché."

———

He called Eva the next day. She felt the same about Caitlin, except she added a couple nouns to Caitlin's list of adjectives: "asshole" and "prick."

They met later at the Alki Tavern to talk. They sat up at the bar.

"Why were you so vindictive with Caiti?" he wanted to know. He was sincerely curious.

"I wasn't vindictive, I told the truth. I have a history of men being assholes to me, and now it seems you are no different."

"You knew I was married."

"It was a mistake, a huge mistake." She peered down into her schooner. "I was attracted to you…and now…I'm in love with you and I don't know what to do about it."

A drunken man was making a ruckus, going from table to table being obnoxious and demanding money for beer. When no one would give him money, he drank the beer sitting in front of people.

"Why is everyone putting up with that asshole?" Eva said.

Peter shrugged.

"Why is no one doing anything? Why isn't the bartender? Why don't *you* do something? Are all the men in here milquetoasts?"

Peter ignored her. The drunk worked his way down the bar, tipping back everyone's beer. He came to Eva, and they watched him pick up Eva's schooner and guzzle it.

It happened so fast hardly anyone saw it. Suddenly the drunk was on the wet floor, and Peter was digging out the drunk's wallet. He picked out a five dollar bill, and then dropped the wallet back onto the prone figure. He put the fiver on the bar. "She'll have another one, Wes," he said to the bartender.

"Jesus, Peter," Wes said.

"What? Oh him? No worries."

Peter reached down and picked up the drunk by the collar with one hand and dragged him across the fir floor and flung him out onto the sidewalk.

Everyone cheered.

"Are you happy now?" he said to Eva.

She stared back open-mouthed. "I hope you didn't hurt him."

The evening pressed on and became like one of their regular dates. Suddenly, she was no longer sad—just happy to be with him.

"I feel so right with you," she said.

Eva and Caitlin were alike this way: one moment viciously angry; the next lovey dovey and kind. It was difficult for him to comprehend this sort of behavior. When he got angry he stayed angry for awhile. He was still angry about the drunk. He had a sudden image of his father coming home and kicking furniture out of his way. Everyone stayed out of his way. He and Perry fled to their rooms, terrified he would come in and slap them around for no reason, other than because he was drunk. It had happened on occasion. He hadn't told his therapist about that. He had forgotten. It occurred to Peter in a sudden revelation that his father had PTSD from his own experiences in war.

"What are you thinking, Peter?"

"I don't know what you want."

"I know you, Peter. I think I know you better than you know yourself. You can't decide on me or Caitlin. You let others decide things for you. You don't finish things: your relationships, your projects, your novel."

He stared at her, angry with her insight.

"Don't you think it's time to follow through on things and make decisions?"

It was two a.m. They had gone to the Alki Inn and had a breakfast of eggs and sausage with whole wheat toast. They strolled down Alki. The bay was black and calm. Waves washed over driftwood in blanketed lumps.

"Do you want to remain unhappily married or not?"

"Things could be worse."

She sighed. "Why couldn't you have been bald and fat?"

"Why couldn't you?"

They laughed.

"Look." The moon appeared from behind a black, yellow rimmed cloud. It was large and bright as a lamp, lighting their way. The bay suddenly beamed bright reflections. They continued their stroll, their arms around each other.

"Being comfortable has a lot to do with it," he said.

"Huh?"

"You know: a house on Alki, a cabin in Lake Chelan; two cars; two TVs."

"Two lovers." Then she nodded as if she now understood. "Yeah, I get that. There have been times in my life I would have given my left tit for a little comfort."

"No big loss." Eva had small breasts.

They laughed. "You asshole. There you go again not being funny."

"You know one reason why I go out with other women?"

"I'm really not interested, Peter."

"Why wouldn't you be interested? It's just one reason. One itsy bitsy reason really."

They laughed. "Okay. What is it?"

"It's the one thing in my life that's interesting. I have a boring life except for that."

She frowned. "You could start and not finish another novel."

"That hurt."

"I didn't mean it. I read your book of short stories, you know. It's what you write about. Your fiction is autobiographical."

———

At home Caitlin was up waiting for him.

"I thought you were just going to talk to her," she said.

"It's all we did, talk."

"And drink," she added in disgust.

"You don't drink, so don't criticize those of us who choose to."

"What is there about drinking that is not open for criticism?"

"It's too late for this…I'm exhausted. I'm talked out. I just want bed."

He started toward the bedroom, but she grabbed him and whirled him around.

"You've been with Eva all night, and you can't give me five minutes?"

"What."

She began to pound on his chest with both fists. She looked up at him in hysterical tears. "*Fuck you!*" She ran off.

———

In the morning he was nursing his hangover with black coffee. The morning paper looked back at him in a blur.

Caitlin sat down across from him at the kitchen table. "So what decision have you come to?"

Why did Eva and Caiti keep pestering him about some monumental decision? Why couldn't they all just get along? It was really becoming too much! More than he could bear! He ignored her and kept reading the paper.

She snatched the paper out from under him. "How can you sit there reading that stupid paper and ignore what's going on?"

"I wasn't aware there was a decision to be made."

"There's your family or there's Eva."

"That doesn't sound like a decision, it sounds like an ultimatum."

"It is. Either you start being a responsible husband and father, or you leave."

He stared at her. "I'm thinking about it."

She stared back. "Thinking about what?"

"I'm thinking about leaving you."

He was not really thinking about leaving her; he just wanted her off his back so he could read the goddamned newspaper in peace.

She stared incredulously, her light Irish blue eyes twinkling with tears. "Are you really?"

"Yes. Can I have my paper back now?"

"And what about the boys?" Before he could answer, she threw the paper in his face and left the room.

———

At school Monday he called Eva and told her what happened.

"Poor Caiti," she said, and sighed. "The woman is sick in love with you. It's obvious she'll do anything to keep you and it's obvious you can get away with anything with her. You can move in with me."

"What?"

"You can move in with me until we decide what to do."

"No!"

"You said you were moving out."

"I said I was thinking about it."

"What's there to think about?"

"Eva, I'm not abandoning my family." There was a pregnant pause. Then he said, "But I don't want to stop seeing you either."

"I can't do it anymore."

"Why not?"

"Because I can't keep doing that to myself, or Caiti."

"I love you."

"No, you don't. I don't think you're capable of loving anyone." She hung up.

But she called right back. "I need to see you."

"When?"

"Tonight. I need to see you tonight."

"I can't tonight."

"*Please.*"

"Eva…I can't tonight."

"When then."

"Maybe tomorrow."

"Tomorrow then."

"We'll see."

He couldn't see her tonight because he wasn't in the mood to deal with her moods. Maybe tomorrow he would be so inclined.

TWENTY-FOUR

The more he drank the more he shot off his mouth. First everyone was laughing with him, then all of a sudden everyone was silent, as if he'd said something wrong.

In the men's room after zipping up with authority, he turned to a man filling the men's room exit doorway.

"McMahon," this very large man muttered. He was missing front teeth.

"Hey," Jackson returned, without a clue as to who he was. He had a crooked smile frozen on a whiskered face. He stood about six-four. He was wide as a barrel.

"How ya doin', McMahon?"

"I'm doin' good, thanks."

"Are ya good for that two hundred you owe me?"

Jackson picked his pack of Camels out of his shirt pocket, jogged a few smokes free from the pack, offering one to this very large man. Long, thick fingers picked out a cigarette carefully, as if looking for a specific one, as if it were a box of chocolates instead of a pack of cigarettes.

Jackson picked one out for himself, brought out his lighter from his pants pocket, lit Very Large Man's cigarette for him, then his own.

"Ya know," Jackson said, exhaling smoke away from his new friend. "I'm tryin' like hell ta remember you, but I'm drawin' a blank."

"Ya don't remember." Very Large Man drew deeply on his cigarette, then looked at it as he exhaled, like a man shopping for the right smoke. "Ya don't have it, I take it."

"200 bucks? No. But I'll buy you a drink."

"McCann."

"Hm?"

"M'name's McCann. And you're McMahon. McCann and McMahon, it's why I remember: word association."

"I'm impressed."

"I never forget a face—or an incident. Two years ago I gave you some coke and you promised to pay me later. I never saw you again of course, until right now. Not that I blame you much, I was dumb to trust you. I had met you just that night. McMahon. That's what I never forgot. Everyone said: 'You loaned money to McMahon?' They laughed. I never forget."

"What's your poison, McCann?"

They were approaching the bar.

"Jack. Straight up."

"Hey, Charlie, two Jack Daniels here. Doubles. No ice."

They drank their drinks, smoked their smokes.

"Hey, McMahon," McCann said. "Wanna buy some coke?"

Jackson looked at him doubtfully.

McCann laughed, his broken-toothed mouth like a black cavern. "Buy some coke! That's a good one, huh, McMahon?"

"Hey, man, I genuinely don't remember you, or the incident. I must have been drunk. I'm not always responsible for myself when I'm drunk."

"So who the fuck is? I kissed that money bye bye long ago! 'I must have been drunk.' That's a good one, McMahon! Of course we were drunk!"

He nudged Jackson playfully, and Jackson stumbled against the guy sitting next to him, causing the guy to spill his drink.

"Sorry," Jackson said to him.

"Why don't ya watch what the fuck you're doin'."

"Sorry," he repeated.

"*Sorry*," he mimicked. "Asshole."

Jackson turned back to his drink.

McCann nudged Jackson into the guy again just as the guy was tipping back his drink, and this time the guy stepped away from the bar with an enraged look, wiping away spilt liquor off his face and the front of his shirt.

"Don't learn, do ya?"

Jackson ignored him. What he thought he saw next was a flash of something over his head, and the guy he was pushed into was suddenly on the floor staring up astonished at the looming, morose, massive figure of McCann.

Charlie the bartender came rushing over. "I'm calling the cops!"

"Come on, little guy." Jackson was lifted off the stool by the collar and pulled outside like a tight bundle of air.

Next he knew he was sitting on the passenger side of a '65 Bonneville, pulling on a crack pipe that McCann was holding his lighter to.

Then McCann lit a rock himself.

"You're just walking trouble, ain't you, McMahon?" McCann said.

"Me?"

"Yeah you. My knuckles hurt."

Jackson laughed. "Let's go. I'll buy you another drink."

So they ventured to another bar, where Jackson ordered two more double Jacks, except this time he discovered himself broke.

———

His head pounding, he stared across an unfamiliar room. He slowly unwound, groaned, farted, rolled, and fell, with a thud to a tan carpet.

"What the fuck!" he heard from another room, and then remembered: McCann.

He sat up, looked around, smacked his dry lips, and pushed himself to a stand with a grunt. He found a bathroom, dropped his drawers, sat on the toilet, and shat his loose bowels. A weak trickle leaked from a swollen bladder, stopped, dribbled, and eventually emptied most of itself while he had a cigarette.

He followed the rich aroma of coffee brewing, and found McCann at a kitchen table slurping at a bowl of cereal, an open box of Fruit Loops on the table.

"Coffee's 'bout done," he said.

Jackson sat down across from him. "What time is it?"

"Time ta get my ass ta work."

"What time we get in last night?"

McCann laughed. "Here." He tossed a sandwich bag at Jackson, inside of which resided little white pills.

"Crisscrosses," Jackson identified.

"Lifesavers, I call 'em."

Jackson opened the glassine bag and removed two, tossing them into his mouth. He poured two cups of java, set one down in front of McCann subserviently, then sat down again across from him.

"Where do you work?" Jackson said.

"Baugh Construction."

Jackson nodded; he'd worked there; he'd worked everywhere.

"I gotta go," he said, standing with his mug. "You can stay until you're ready to go."

And just like that, he had a new friend and a place to stay. It always happened like that. There was an aura of spirituality about it. We're all connected like a web, the Buddha said.

After McCann left, the speed kicked in. He finished loading the dishwasher, wiped the counter clean, then sat with a smoke and ruminated.

Deciding he should eat, he looked in the fridge for something palatable, saw a half gallon of whole milk, a half empty bottle of ketchup, and five tall Buds. He uncapped a Bud, and washed his dry throat.

He grabbed another and decided to explore the premises. In the bedroom the queen sized bed was neat as a pin. The closet was stacked with clothes, arranged in formation on the hangers: Suits, sweaters, shirts, then pants.

Feeling a bit chilly, he picked a goose down vest off a hanger and tried it on, inspecting himself in the full-length mirror. *Large*, he acceded, *but what the fuck, that's the style these days.*

He returned to the kitchen for another beer, sitting back down in a kitchen chair to sip it at a leisurely pace. The sandwich bag of amphetamines was still on the kitchen table. He slipped it into the pocket of the down vest. He finished the beer with a flourish. After three beers and a rush of speed, he was feeling pretty damn good.

He saw a Jansport backpack in the living room hanging on a coat rack. He searched its contents and found only a pack of Marlboros.

His own backpack lost somewhere within the blackout of the previous evening, he marched through the house on a mission, placing items of value into the pack: a gold ring much too large for Jackson's fingers, a gold Rolex watch much too large for Jackson's wrist, a gold necklace. In the medicine cabinet he discovered a vial of Percocet, prescribed to a Robert McCann for back pain. He tossed that into the backpack as well, but not before tossing two into his mouth. In the spare bedroom he rummaged through an antique chest of drawers and found an unwrinkled wallet so new it had that fresh tanned leather smell. Inside were five crisp one hundred dollar bills. Into the backpack it went.

Back in the kitchen he enjoyed the last beer. He stared dreamily out the front window at a territorial view he tried, but failed, to recognize. He assumed it was Seattle, but exactly where he hadn't a clue.

He felt perfect. A hit of speed, a couple of Percocet, and a few mellow beers had put him in a rare state of transcendence. If only he could capture this feeling indefinitely, he wouldn't be an addict. But that was the whole problem: in too little time this divine state would begin to abate, and he would instead reside in a desperate quest to recapture it, and in doing so lose the initial euphoria in uncontrollable inebriation.

His whole issue with sobriety was that this transcendent state of consciousness that he appreciated this very moment in which all suffering, physical and emotional, ceased, could not exist. In sobriety comes suffering.

He finished the last beer, had a nice toxin-purging pee, tried the backpack on with a little shrug of his shoulders, opened the front door to a brisk whip of morning wind, looked from left to right as if to embark on a mission impossible, and shut the door behind him after assuring it was locked: *Wouldn't want any burglars easy access, ha ha.*

TWENTY-SIX

Jackson was sitting in a bar striking up a conversation with the only other customer beside himself, a woman by the name of Jane, with long, curly, reddish brown hair, light gray eyes, a bit thick around the hips, and an amazing mass of dotted brown freckles that spread over her face as if someone had splattered a mud ball over it. This latter feature actually added interest to her rather than diminishing it. She was pretty, he decided.

These fascinating freckles extended to another part of her anatomy, he observed later from another viewpoint, in her small apartment in the Greenwood district of Seattle.

They'd snorted up the coke purchased from the benevolence of McCann's cash, and they were drinking up a fifth of bourbon also purchased from this same cash.

It was the first time he'd had sex since he couldn't remember when, and he'd been making the most of it all afternoon.

"Spank me?" she suggested diplomatically, as he continued to bounce off her ample bum pacing himself like a marathon man, a puddle of sweat building in the small of her back.

He began with patty cakes, gradually increasing his tempo until he eventually was raising purplish welts as she cried out in pain, then he cried out himself in ecstasy, collapsing beside her, heaving for oxygen, his second orgasm that day: amazing.

While he sat up against the bed stand smoking, she talked and swirled bourbon. He was impressed with her capacity for alcohol, as he witnessed her down two shots for his every one, a feat seldom observed.

She talked about two ex-husbands and young children in the custody of said husbands, a monstrous injustice perpetrated by an obviously male-biased judicial system, she pontificated with indignation, and drank. Jackson nodded empathetically.

He asked her if he could shower. She directed him to the bathroom, where he took a long, hot shower, afterwards borrowing her razor to shave. He felt much better.

All scrubbed to a pink shine, he exited the bathroom to find Jane had disappeared. There was a note on the bed that said, "Gone for food, be right back."

He snatched the TV remote, flicked through the channels, landing on a Mariners game, sat back with another shot of bourbon, another cigarette, and the ball game: heaven.

She came bounding in, freckled cheeks rosy from the brief brush with September's brisk elements, carrying a McDonald's bag, from which she produced two bacon cheeseburgers, two orders of fries, and two large cokes.

Jackson emptied what was left of the bourbon into the cokes equally, and they sat back with their repast and watched the game.

While eating she said to him: "You sure can fuck."

"Yeah?" He laughed, appreciating the compliment.

"Not that I'm any expert, I'm only 28. I've had two husbands and six lovers. One nighters don't count, do they?"

"I've never counted 'em."

"They were all bad enough not to count. 'Wham bam, ma'am, get me a beer.' One guy I went out with for awhile though—he kept on pumping till he'd come again, never losing his hardon. But he was an asshole. He was a college professor and he was married."

Jackson looked at her with a startled interest and wondered. *No, no,* he thought, *too coincidental,* while keeping his eyes posted on the game, bottom of the 8th, tied 2 to 2. For the moment he'd lost the inclination to drink.

"Then there's Joey, the handsomest of the bunch. He was beautiful. Six-foot-three if he was an inch, eyes like violets; he coulda been a model. He had a good job at Boeing, twenty plus bucks an hour, took me out all the time to dinner, movies, drinking. But he never wanted to fuck! I went with him for two months and I think we fucked twice. It was too frustrating. Sex is important to me. He came over one day and caught me in bed with another guy. Exit Joey. I sorta miss him; he was so pleasant to look at. He spent two hours a day in the gym lifting weights. Too tired to fuck, I guess."

Jackson picked out his last cigarette, crumpled the empty pack in his fist and dropped it into an ashtray. "Do you have any cigarettes?"

"Don't smoke," she said, shaking her head vigorously to emphasize the fact. "Quit ten years ago when I was pregnant with my first. Them things will kill ya, lover."

"What can I say? I'm addicted."

"There a 7-Eleven around the corner on 85th."

He dodged garbage on the floor working his way to the bathroom to pee. *How could anyone stand to live in this dump?* he pondered standing over the toilet, forgetting for the moment that this dump was more than what he had to live in, which was nothing. It suddenly dawned on him: *I'm homeless.*

Returning to the bedroom to observe that the Mariners had lost as usual, 3 to 2, he said: "Let's go out."

He slipped on the backpack, and they scooted out the door, down the street to the closest bar.

Outside the bar loitered four youths, 16 years of age at the most. One asked: "Buy us some beer?"

"Sure," Jackson obliged. "What do you want?"

"A case of Rainier Ice," he said, handing Jackson a twenty dollar bill.

Jackson grabbed the twenty, said, "Be right back, guys."

Inside the bar, Jane said rhetorically: "You can be arrested buying alcohol for minors."

"So who's buying alcohol for minors?" he said, slapping the twenty the boy had given him on the bar. "Two bourbons," he ordered.

Jane stared at him. "What about those kids?"

"What kids?"

An hour later they sat in a booth roaring drunk.

"Two more bourbons here!" Jackson called out.

"Yeah, yeah, I'm coming."

"Are ya breathin' hard?" Jackson called out, and Jane found this uproariously funny.

The bartender brought them their drinks. "I'm cutting you off after this."

"That's what she said," Jackson said, and Jane cracked up over this one too.

"Hope you two ain't drivin'," the bartender said, not laughing.

"No, you're drivin'," Jackson said, "drivin' us to another bar!"

Jane was in stitches. She was on her back in the booth grabbing her gut. The bartender resumed duties in what would now be an empty bar.

They swallowed their drinks, stumbled out the door, turned right, and out from the side of the building suddenly emerged four youths.

"Oh shit," Jane said, and instantly turned to run in the opposite direction.

TWENTY-SEVEN

The smell of ammonia tickled his nose. His mouth was dry, and he smacked his lips. He opened his eyes. He saw, but his mind was a blank. There was a constant drone. All was white, a blurry white. He turned to an elderly man in a bed beside him, eyes closed with labored breathing. Both of them were covered with a white blanket. He was sweating and threw it off. He felt movement on the other side, and turned to it. Stepping into his vision was Caitlin.

"How are you feeling?"

He smacked his lips again. "Thirsty."

He motioned to sit up and noticed that he was hooked up to an IV. "What's this?"

Caitlin reappeared with a paper cup with a straw. "You were badly dehydrated."

"Where am I?"

"Harborview Hospital. You got beat up. The bartender from the bar you were at said four youths beat you up. When he yelled at them, they grabbed your backpack and ran."

"Jesus." He draped his hand over his forehead. "Jesus."

"What? What is it?"

"I'm in fucking *pain*."

She rang for a nurse. She sat down next to him and placed her hand softly on his chest.

In a few minutes a nurse appeared.

"He's in pain."

"What kind of pain?"

"The kind of pain someone has when his head is bashed in and his ribs are broken."

"I'm in *fucking pain*," Jackson elaborated.

"I'll talk to the doctor," she said.

"Jacky, they did blood tests."

He nodded, grimacing in pain.

"You need medication to get through withdrawals. You need to get into rehab when you get out."

He nodded again. It wasn't the first time he'd been through this.

"This is serious, Jacky. Your liver, kidneys, and heart are in bad shape."

The nurse appeared again to put Demerol in his IV.

Jackson opened his eyes, looked at Caitlin, felt the drug ease him into a heavenly release, and closed his eyes again.

TWENTY-EIGHT

After six weeks in rehab his ribs were healing, he was fatter than ever, he was rested and ready—and ready to get the hell out.

He'd had three ample meals a day with snacks in between, he'd improved his ping pong game considerably, and he'd watched the Mariners lose to the Yankees in six games for the American League championship. *Damn Yankees.* He hated them when he was a kid; hated them now. He'd been a Dodgers fan. Hank Aaron was the best ever. But they always lost to the Yankees and that goddamned Mickey Mantle.

He sat across from Jim, the pock faced counselor who looked ten years older than his 55 years, who said to Jackson now:

"Ready for the world?"

"Best I've felt in years."

Jim nodded, staring at Jackson uncomfortably. His bright blue eyes were buried behind feathered folds of loose skin; wrinkles etched his cheeks like rivulets, his lumpy head shaved bald, his ears twisted like an old wrestler. A thick gray mustache hid his thin mouth, which held worn out old dentures that clicked like steel every time he shut his mouth, which was seldom. He rode a Harley to work.

He said: "You'll be back within a year."

"Yeah?"

He nodded. "Or more likely, dead."

"Thanks for the encouragement, Jim. They could use more a' that 'round here."

"Just goin' by the stats."

Jackson just stared. What was there to say?

"Ever read any Buddhism?" Jim said.

"No, but I have read *The Wit and Wisdom of Yogi Berra.*"

Jim slapped a dog-eared paperback on his desk. "Here. Take it. It's a gift."

Jackson lifted it off the desk and flipped through the ragged torn pages filled with yellow highlighted passages.

"Gee, Jim, I don't know what to say."

"Read it, don't read it, it's just an idea, no big deal."

"I see you've read it, 'bout twenty times it looks like." He looked at the title: *The Way of Zen* by Alan Watts. "He's a Buddhist?"

"He was. He's dead now. He was an alcoholic, and he killed himself because of it."

"Did a lot for him then, huh?" Jackson said sarcastically, flipping through the pages again.

"He was a Buddhist, but he was also human."

"So what did Buddhism do for him, or for you, for that matter?"

"I used to be a millionaire."

Jackson laughed. "Used to be? That makes my question even more relevant."

"I was financially rich, yes. But spiritually, I was penniless as a pauper. I was lost, unhappy, living my life in a drunken void. I cheated on my wife, cheated personal friends out of thousands of dollars, and was drunk every day. It's all about karma."

"I know karma. You live your life like Richard Nixon and come back as a cockroach. And there are a lot of cockroaches in the world."

"It's even simpler than that, Jackson. You rob a bank, you go to prison. You cheat on your wife, she divorces you. You overindulge in alcohol, your liver rots. You treat yourself and others well, you are rewarded with a healthy constitution and the reciprocation of healthy relationships."

"I don't need a complicated religious philosophy to tell me that."

"And yet people continue to rob banks, cheat on their spouses, and abuse alcohol even when it's killing them."

"Maybe in my next life…"

"There's only this life, Jackson, and it's all an illusion."

"Now you are sounding like a Buddhist."

Jim smiled. Jim never smiled.

"Do you meditate, and all that?"

"I'm a student of Buddhism, but I don't always practice it in my life like I should. I don't even know if I believe in it. But it's helped me."

"Do you advise all your students to study Buddhism?"

"No, but I see a lot of you in me. I think there's an innate spiritual part of you that can be tapped. I was about your age when I quit drinking. My life was worn out; I'd hit bottom. I was tired and ready to die. That was fifteen years ago, after thirty years of hard drinking.

"I've seen enough drunks to know which ones leave here determined to stay sober and which can't get outa here fast enough to hit the nearest bar."

"And which one of these am I?"

"I think you use rehab to get yourself healthy enough to embark on another bout of abuse, until you end up in a hospital, jail, or rehab again. But you've run out of time, Jackson, your body won't recover as it has in the past, it's progressive. But there's a part of you that wants to stay sober and doesn't know it."

Jim stood to refill his coffee mug. He gestured to Jackson with the pot, but Jackson declined the offer with a shudder, as if to say: "Swill arsenic?"

"Your physical cravings have survived for now. You're on your way to a potentially more spiritually fulfilled life. But it's all up here." He tapped his own head with a crippled arthritic finger. "You want to die. Drinking for us is suicidal."

Jackson again thumbed through the book, with only slightly more sincerity this time. "So, what happened to your millions?"

"I gave it back to the people I stole it from."

"What people?"

"People. People like you. Homeless people. Hungry people. Unlucky people. Now I'm here ferrying people across the river."

TWENTY-NINE

Jackson was sharing an old house rotting on its foundation on Capitol Hill. There were a few spindly pine trees in the back, pillars of peeling yellow on the rotting front porch. The house was dust-filled and cramped, shared with five other recovering drunks, noisy with activity. There had been seven of them, but poor old Simple Simon whom everyone loved dearly went on a one-nighter and made the fatal mistake of coming home before he'd sobered up. He was probably out on the streets somewhere right now, sleeping out in the cold November rain.

Jackson hadn't touched a drop in nine weeks. He couldn't say that he'd never drink again, but he wasn't drinking today. He would occasionally sneak out and grab a few tokes off a pipe though. He'd gone through many dry periods throughout his 25 years of hard drinking, but the one mind-altering indulgency he'd never seemed able to give up was marijuana.

He'd read that book Jim had given him, and it had interested him enough to walk over to the local library and check out another book of Buddhism from the early part of the Twentieth Century by D. J. Suzuki. He had never before been one for religious themes. Jesus was cool, but he hadn't been able to make sense of the contradictory lessons of the Old Testament with the New, or of a supposedly loving God that allowed so much suffering. Buddhism said that life *is* suffering, so get used to it. And Buddhism wasn't so much religious, far as he could tell, or even philosophical, as it was spiritual musings that had at least some semblance of rationale.

Sitting in the living room with the others watching a Sonics game, Henry, reading *The Seattle Times* said, "No one's claimed a $12 million Lotto ticket from September 2nd."

"Shit," Jackson said, not about the lotto ticket, but about the fact that Vin Baker was 0 for 5 from the field, missing another five footer.

A thought undulated through the damaged synapses and split neurons of Jackson's wet brain, and he reached to his behind for his thick worn out wallet, getting it out and thumbing through the tidbits of receipts, unpaid bills, and whatnot until he found the Lotto ticket. Reading the date, it was—interestingly enough—September 2. "Huh."

"Whataya got there, Jackson," Ski said, "the winning ticket?" and laughed.

Jackson held it out to the room for display. Henry's curiosity piqued, he stood laboriously and pushed his bloated and battered 300-pound, 54-year-old body away from the sofa and shuffled over to pick the ticket away from Jackson's trembling hand. He stared fascinated for a moment, mouth open; breathing labored from the shuffle across the room, then looked at Jackson. "There are six numbers circled here, all in a row."

Jackson said, "Let me see that paper."

He compared the numbers.

"What's the numbers say?" Ski said, glancing back and forth between Jackson and the game.

"I'll be damned."

THIRTY

Jackson got off the bus on Fauntleroy Way SW, walked past the Gatewood Elementary School where'd he'd long ago played basketball and baseball with Hoge and his brothers. By the looks of things it hadn't been maintained much over the years, the asphalt corroded and cracked, sprouting weeds. He couldn't imagine anyone playing on it anymore. The three story brick structure looked as if it could use some maintenance as well, with broken windows and loose mortar in the old brick. There seemed to be no money for working class neighborhoods anymore.

He ambled past the Lincoln Park tennis courts where he and Hoge had played on as kids, and still had on occasion until their drinking affected their physical condition enough to neutralize any desire they had left for physical activity.

It was a sunny day, unusually warm, and the courts were filled to capacity with people waiting. The theatrics of tennis players like John McEnroe, Jimmy Connors, and Ilie Nastashe had produced a tennis boom, a sudden interest in recreational tennis. There apparently was enough money in the public coffers to maintain the tennis courts. *Oh well, tennis was more popular than school.*

He walked up the broken concrete path to Mrs. Hogan's front door, noticing the house hadn't changed much since he was a kid, many coated layers of dark gray paint over the old cedar shakes.

His pickup was gone from where he had left it in her driveway. He had to remember to ask about that. She'd probably had it towed away. Not that he could blame her. But the old pickup was a classic, and with a little work he could have it back in running order.

He knocked on the door, and the immediate response was a dog's deep, vicious bark. But when the door was cracked open enough to stretch the door chain taut, a friendly wet snout poked through, sniffed and whimpered. Rex remembered him.

"Yes?" Mrs. Hogan said.

"It's Jacky McMahon, Mrs. Hogan."

"Hello, Jacky." She unlatched the chain and opened the door wide.

Rex jumped up on him, tail wagging, long tongue hanging lazily out the right side of his snout. "Hey, boy!" Jackson said, laughing, petting him. On his back two legs, he was as tall as Jackson, and probably weighed as much.

"Down, Rex! Bad dog! Down!"

Rex ignored the order, and Jackson put the German shepherd down on all fours, but he jumped right back up.

"Down, Rex!" she repeated. "Bad dog!"

"It's all right, Mrs. Hogan, I'm glad to see him."

"He knows he's not s'ppse to do that. How are you, Jacky?"

"I'm well, Mrs. Hogan. And you?"

Mrs. Hogan had to be in her late sixties by now, and looked even older in her long, unfashionable, rust-colored dress. It came to about two inches above her ankles. Her gaze was pleasant and lively. As a kid, he'd had a crush on her, with her laughing blue eyes and shoulder length reddish brown hair. The house held five males in those days: Her husband Dave, who had killed himself driving his car drunk into a telephone pole one night when Hoge was sixteen; Hoge and his three other brothers, two older, and one younger. One older brother fell asleep in a two-bit hotel one night with a cigarette and died from smoke inhalation when he was 26. The oldest brother was a good enough golfer to be a tour pro, but lacked a sponsor from his humble background, and so became a golf hustler in Las Vegas. He apparently had hustled hundreds of thousands off people like Michael Jordon and Charles Barkley. But then apparently he hustled the wrong person, and his body was discovered on the 18th green, shot through the head. Hoge's younger brother was the one "success story," apparently doing well with his own construction business, but he was estranged from the family, and wouldn't even contact his own mother.

While no longer attractive, Mrs. Hogan with her white hair and clean unmade up face still had a pleasant and calm demeanor, durable if not full of the vitality and constitution she'd once maintained against a challenging home environment.

They were having coffee and chocolate chip cookies.

"Johnny isn't here," she said, nudging the plate of cookies to him. "Sorry they're not home made. Don't have anyone to bake for no more."

"Do you know where he is?" Jackson said, reaching for another cookie. "I have something important for him."

"I doubt that he's alive, Jacky." She sipped her coffee stoically and stared out the side window. "He was drinking up my Social Security check. He was killing himself, and I couldn't take it anymore. I told him he had to leave, and he left."

"You don't know where he went?"

She shook her head. "I did call around to some old friends, worried about him, but no one knows."

"When was that?"

"Weeks ago. He's disappeared."

Jackson nibbled the cookie reflectively. He wasn't sure what to do. "Well then," he said, getting out his wallet. "I guess this belongs to you."

He picked out the wrinkled Lotto ticket and tossed it dismissively on the coffee table, as if to be rid of it.

"What's that?"

"When we were living together he came home one night with this Lotto ticket. It's worth twelve million dollars."

"That's not funny, Jacky."

"I'm not kidding, Mrs. Hogan. You're rich. I went over the numbers over and over. It's from September 2. There was one winner, and no one's claimed it."

She carefully picked it up and stared at the numbers as if they were an incomprehensible math problem. "But I didn't purchase it."

"No, Johnny did."

"But you were living with him at the time. It's yours."

"You're the closest living relative."

"I don't want it. What would I do with all that money?" She now held it out at arm's length as if the little snip of paper was virulent. "I don't want it."

"Somebody has to claim it soon, or the money goes back to the general fund."

"Either you take it right now, or I tear it apart." She held it out to him.

"Why don't you want it?"

"What am I going to do with twelve million dollars? I wouldn't even know where to start. I have my Social Security and my pension, and I have no one to give it too, other than you. So you keep it. Do good things with it."

Jackson ate another cookie and drained his coffee. The ticket now lay on the coffee table like a burden no one wanted to take on. He had read somewhere that the majority of lottery winners eventually filed for bankruptcy. Why? There seemed an element of karma in getting rich that suddenly. That yin and yang thing again.

He slowly, guiltily, picked the ticket up and held it loosely between the thumbs and forefingers of both hands, about to tear it in two.

He quickly returned it to his wallet.

"There is one thing you can do for me, Jacky," she said.

"Name it, Mrs. Hogan."

"Would you please get that old pickup off my property?"

"Where is it? I didn't see it."

"I had Jimmy push it behind the house out of sight."

THIRTY-ONE

Jackson set his toolbox in front of the old pickup and popped open the rusty hood. It was like a military press pushing it open. A freezing chill from the long stagnant truck's steel structure radiated across his face like the brush of a ghost.

He oiled the hinges with 3 in 1 oil. He put the battery on a battery charger. He drained the oil, coal black, thick with engine debris splashing into the pan. He replaced the oil filter, air filter, and fuel filter; replaced the spark plugs, wires, and distributor. He replaced the starter motor. He poured fresh oil into the crank case. He put water in the battery. The entire process took him almost three hours.

He took it off the battery charger and stepped back, wiping his hands with a grease rag. He lit a cigarette. Stepping into the frigid cab with the cigarette dangling from the side of his mouth, he crossed the fingers of his left hand for good luck and turned the ignition key. After one laborious churn, to his pleasant surprise the engine turned over—coughed, spit, sparks conducted, and pistons started jumping. A puff of blue smoke emitted from the exhaust, and the engine came to life.

He allowed it to idle while he put all his tools in his brand new tool box and put the tool box and battery charger into the creosoted wood bed.

He took an envelope out of his pocket. Inside the envelope was a check made out to Adele Hogan for $10,000. He put the envelope in the mailbox.

He got into the cab of his truck, pumped the accelerator a few times, placed the manual transmission into reverse to the tune of an old familiar clunk, and eased out the driveway.

He drove to Peter and Caiti's and left an envelope in their mailbox. He drove to his parents and left one in their mailbox. He drove to Josephine's and—though he'd heard she was still drinking—left a check with her regardless.

It was just the beginning of his plan to pay everyone back. There were many ex- friends he had borrowed from and not paid back over the years, and he planned on paying them all back if he could, with interest. He also wanted to pay McCann back the money he stole from him, but he couldn't remember where he lived; somewhere in the north end, but he couldn't be sure, he was so out of it at the time. He tried calling all the McCann's in the Seattle phone book, but had no luck.

———

The house he paid cash for was a small one bedroom bungalow six blocks east of Lincoln Park, alongside a steep street called Holly. There was a small kitchen with old, weathered oak cabinets, and a half-sized refrigerator, the linoleum old and cracked. There was no dishwasher. He enjoyed washing dishes by hand; it was meditative. There was one bathroom. The bedroom was barely large enough for a single bed. In the living room was a small sofa and chair facing an old Den Franklin wood burning stove. The central heating was oil.

In the yard there were two nearly one-hundred-foot tall Douglas fir and one Western Red Cedar nearly as tall. A rotting six-foot cedar fence surrounded about a quarter acre of land. He needed a fenced in yard because he now had a dog, a black lab mix rescued from the Animal Shelter whom he named Joeboy.

This morning he was loading the pickup with his brand new 16" bar Stihl chain saw, a new splitting mall, axe, his tool box, chain oil, gas can mixed with gas and two-cycle oil, a back pack with a thermos of coffee and a lunch of sandwiches and cookies, and a paperback called *Simple Zen*.

Joeboy jumped into the passenger side eagerly and they headed out east on Fauntleroy Way SW onto the West Seattle Bridge, turned north onto I-5 for the quarter mile cutoff east onto I-90, over the floating bridge, past Mercer Island and Bellevue.

On his left Sammamish whizzed by. He remembered skinny dipping there one night with Peter and some girls they had picked up in Bellevue. It had then been a plush haven of marsh and crystal blue water, and now the shores were polluted with dense condominiums.

Past Sammamish, to North Bend and cragged Mount Si visible to the left, which he and Peter had climbed at least twenty times, back in the day when he could appreciate physical exertion with the knowledge that afterwards came the reward: alcohol. From now on any reward from physical activity would have to be only the increased fitness of the physical body.

Up Snoqualmie Pass he drove until the cutoff assigned to him by the Forest Service, turning left onto a bumpy Weyerhaeuser logging road.

He accelerated slowly in first gear inspecting the ruined landscape. The once pristine terrain that had been thick with biodiversity was now strewn with stumps and slash, piles of branches from drying pyramids alongside the road. He had his pick. He pulled up alongside one of these piles and parked.

He let Joeboy out to pee and explore.

It was cold, close to freezing. His breath blew funnels of crystal frost. He slipped on his fur-lined leather work gloves. He lit a cigarette and circled the pile of slash identifying various species of alder, fir, and cedar—the later of which was worthless for his wood burning stove other than as kindling.

He lifted the chain saw from the back of the pickup. As he was doing so someone else drove up in a late model Ford pickup.

"Howdy," he said, pulling up and rolling down his window.

"Hello!"

"Looks like we got easy pickings today."

Jackson nodded, looking around.

"Like your truck," he said, looking it over.

"Thanks."

"'66?"

"'65." Jackson was pouring a canister of 2-cycle oil into the gas can.

The man in the Ford continued to stare for a moment, then said, "Happy cutting."

"You too." Jackson smiled at him good-naturedly, shaking his can vigorously to mix oil and gas.

He fueled the chain saw and topped off the chain oil chamber. After plugging his ear canal with foam ear protectors, he pumped the oil plug a few times, pulled out the choke, and pulled on the rope starter. It started right up.

Three hours later he had cut, split, and stacked the wood into his pickup. He was beat. His friend two piles over was still cutting.

Jackson poured coffee from his thermos and sat on the tailgate eating a cheddar cheese sandwich and looking across the Cascade Range. It was a beautiful day, and he was no longer cold. The mountaintops glistened with blinding bright snow. He was worn out. He yearned for a beer. The smell of the coffee and the taste of his cigarette was no help. Joeboy sat before him begging food. He tossed him the crust.

The other man broke from his labor and got a thermos out of his cab. He walked carefully over the spongy top soil toward Jackson. He was about thirty, with cropped hair and a neatly trimmed beard. He wore a red-checked flannel shirt and Lee jeans held up with suspenders.

"All loaded?"

Jackson nodded, swinging his head around to look at the load as if to confirm the results of his labor.

"Didn't take long."

"New chain saw." He smiled. "Went through the logs like butter."

"Nice." The man looked back at his own labor. "I gotta sharpen my chain."

"Ah."

The man looked at Jackson's chain saw as if thinking about taking it. "How 'bout some Seagram's in that coffee?" he said instead.

Jackson looked at the bottle in his hand. "No thanks."

Uninvited, he joined Jackson on the tail gate and poured whiskey into his metal cup.

"Kind of a shame what they're doin' to this countryside," he said.

Jackson nodded in vague agreement, looking around at the raped terrain.

"Oh well, can't stop progress. Where ya from?"

"Seattle."

He nodded. "I live about five miles from here, in Snoqualmie."

"Pretty town." Jackson drained his coffee cup, and poured more. He lit a cigarette, offering one to his new friend. He took one.

"What do you do?" he asked Jackson.

"I'm retired."

"No shit. You one a them retired Microsoft millionaires?"

Jackson laughed. "No."

"Married?"

"No."

"Lucky for you. Me, I'm goin' through a divorce. Went home early from work one day and found my wife in bed with my best friend."

Jackson was guiltily reminded of the time a friend found him in bed with the friend's wife.

He put the thermos back into his backpack. Joeboy jumped into the cab of the pickup as if sensing it was time to go and didn't want to be left behind. He offered chocolate chip cookies to his new friend with his open sandwich bag. He declined, and sipped his whiskey.

"A week ago my ol' lady moved in with the ex-best friend right after I got laid off from my job."

"Man," Jackson sympathized, at the same time wondering why he was telling him all this.

Joeboy jumped out of the cab to see what was going on, and now sat in front of him begging again. Jackson tossed him a cookie.

"Oh well, life sucks an' if you're lucky ya die young," he said, offering his right hand. "I'm George."

Jackson took hold of his hand. "Jacky."

"You wouldn't want to buy my load of firewood, wouldja?"

Jackson shook out his empty sandwich bag of crumbs over Joeboy's head. "How much?"

"I can get a full cord in my bed with the side rails. One-fifty?"

"You'd have to drive it to West Seattle."

"That's okay."

"All right then."

Jackson wrote his address on a piece of paper and explained how to get there.

"You wouldn't happen to have a sharpening file, would you? I can return it when I get to your place."

Jackson nodded, and got the sharpening file out of his toolbox, handing it over to George.

"One other thing, I'm outa gas. If you can loan me forty bucks we can subtract it from the one-fifty when I get to your place."

Jackson got two twenties out of his wallet, and handed it over.

"I'd sure get the job done quicker if I borrowed that new chain saw a yours."

Jackson thought about this, and then shrugged. "All right."

As Jackson drove slowly away over the bumpy logging road he spotted George in the rear view mirror standing beside the new Stihl chain saw pouring more whiskey into his cup.

———

He stopped at a North Bend café for coffee. Outside the café was a Jeep Cherokee with a four point deer strapped securely on the roof rack. Inside the café were four men sitting at a booth laughing loudly and talking all at once, with large breakfasts set in front of them. They were drinking beer.

Jackson swallowed back a nearly irresistible urge to order a beer and instead ordered a double short latte to go, and left behind a five dollar tip in the tip jar. The woman behind the bar didn't respond to this generous tip in any particular manner, looking as if she'd rather be anywhere than here.

Jackson sat on the bench outside the café with his latte having a cigarette. He felt depressed. He felt that he had left himself behind somewhere, and the guy sitting here was someone else. He listened to the loud voices of the hunters in the café behind him. There was a refreshing odor of imminent rain. He flipped open *Simple Zen*.

A woman appeared suddenly before him. She looked about his age, but he then thought she was probably younger. It was getting harder to tell people's age as he himself got older. Her hair was stringy and greasy. She was thin and unhealthy looking, but somewhere within this outer façade was an attractive woman.

"I'm broke an' I need to get to Seattle," she said, point blank.

Jackson got out his wallet, took out a crisp twenty, and placed it neatly into her outstretched, trembling hand.

"You wouldn't happen ta be headin' that way, would ya?"

Jackson nodded. "Lessgo."

She followed him to the pickup. When she opened the door she was taken aback by Joeboy, who stared back at her stupidly. She got in, nudging him to the middle. "Nice doggy."

He turned onto I-90. Rain began to splatter the windshield.

"Do you have a cigarette?" she said.

He got out his cigarettes from his vest pocket and saw that he had only two left in the pack. He took one for himself, and then handed her the pack. She searched out the lone cigarette and put the empty package beside her on the seat. He lit hers and then his own.

She blew smoke out a crack in the window. "You want it here, or you wanna pull over."

Jackson glanced at her nonplussed. "What?" He wondered if she planned on shooting him.

"Your blowjob."

He looked back and forth from her to the highway. "I don't want a blowjob."

She shrugged indifferently, puffed, looked out the window following Mount Si as it glided by. "For another twenty I'll give you a 'specially good one, the best you'll ever get…an' I swallow."

Jackson's desire to drink was momentarily replaced with a more primal urge.

He pulled over.

———

When he got home he unloaded the firewood from the pickup, stacking it in the wood shed he'd just built.

George never showed. Karma.

THIRTY-TWO

Turning off the West Seattle Bridge northbound onto 1-5, on the right side of the freeway is a greenbelt that stretches for several miles toward downtown Seattle where once homeless people had established pockets of tent shelters. This is city property, and the homeless compound was tolerated by the city for several years. But then Mayor Paul Schell—probably more concerned with maintaining an image of prosperity in Seattle than finding solutions for the homeless problem—announced that the encampment was a health hazard and dispatched his official police goons to chase the homeless people away and then cleared the encampments.

This group of about fifty homeless individuals had nowhere to go and decided en masse to stay together in solidarity wherever they went. They travelled to various locales setting up their tents, but Paul Schell's Gestapo was right behind, chasing them away, forcing them to keep moving. Schell and the rest of the City Council were probably hoping they would just disappear, but instead, this nomadic group of unified individuals attracted the attention of the local media. A private landowner, who became aware of the situation, donated a portion of his acreage for the homeless to set up a Tent City. Strict rules were enforced in the camp outlawing alcohol, drugs, and fighting. It seemed a temporary solution had been found.

But Mayor Schell—not to be outdone by solutions—dug out some archaic zoning code law, and again forced the homeless legion to move on.

Then, Robert Mateus, director of *El Centro de la Raza*, a community based Chicano/Latin civil rights organization, donated their parking lot to the homeless group, and another Tent City was established.

Schell told Mateus that he couldn't allow the Tent City to remain on the property, but Mateus ignored him. Subsequently, daily fines were levied against *El Centro do la Raza* until such time that he would remove the encampment. Mateus remained defiant, and as the fines tallied into the thousands of dollars, Mateus told the Tent City people that as long as the rules against alcohol, drugs, and fighting were enforced, and they kept the encampment clean, they could stay until permanent housing was provided for them.

Caitlin decided to provide a breakfast day for the Tent City. She called around to friends and acquaintances asking for help and donations.

On the morning of the breakfast, Jackson pulled his pickup in front of Peter and Caitlin's house to load it with food, clothing, tents, and an old Weber barbecue. She rode with him to Beacon Hill and *El Centro de la Raza* where already friends and acquaintances were there getting ready to set up their breakfast.

On the way Jackson asked how Peter was doing, and she said he was fine.

"Really?"

"Yes." She looked at him "Why?"

Jackson shrugged.

"Okay, he's going through one of his 'moods'," she admitted.

"Moods?"

"It's what he calls them. I call it depression."

"Is he still taking his meds?"

"That's the thing. He stopped."

"Did he say why?"

"He said he didn't like how they made him feel. He said they made him feel tired and even more depressed, and kept him from writing."

"And how's that going?"

"His writing? I don't know."

"He's not writing?"

"He's always writing. I just don't know what about."

"Is he still working on his novel about Vietnam?"

She nodded.

"Have you read it?"

She looked at him. "Some of it."

"And?"

"It's very good, brilliant in fact...But..."

"But?"

"I'm no literary critic..."

"It's difficult?"

"It's difficult to understand what he's doing. It's not like a novel at all; it's like a series of short stories that have no connection to one another."

"Oh well." Jackson shrugged. "He's the writer."

"Yes, I'm sure he knows what he's doing, but he never seems satisfied with it and is constantly revising. And another thing..."

"What?"

"Sometimes he goes into these trances."

"Trances?"

"Yes. Like yesterday, he hadn't come upstairs from his study, so I went down to check on him, and he was just sitting there staring at the wall. When I called out to him he didn't answer. Then I shook him, and he came out of it."

"How often does *that* happen?"

"It's happened a few times throughout our marriage. Not often."

Jackson stared thoughtfully out the window. "And women?"

She didn't answer right away, and he thought she was going to ignore the question, but then she said: "I've gotten used to that."

"Oh, Cait." He put a hand on her thigh, until it looked as if she was going to cry, so he took it away and looked out the passenger window. "Is he still drinking?"

"Yes."

"I bet if the drinking stopped, so would the womanizing."

She looked at him. "You think I haven't thought of that? Do you think he's an alcoholic?"

"If his drinking is a problem with you, it's a problem with him."

"It doesn't seem to affect him physically. He seems to metabolize it with his exercise program."

"That won't last forever."

They arrived at the Tent City. It was cold, but another beautiful day. Several of the Tent City people eagerly rushed up to help Jackson and Caitlin unload the supplies.

Caitlin told Jackson she needed him to drive to Salty's on Alki to see a man by the name of Joe. Salty's was donating food for the breakfast.

"I'll go with you," said a large man six foot plus and a good 300 pounds, wearing a sweat lined cowboy hat and faded blue overalls. In the pickup the big man introduced himself as Mark.

"We really appreciate what you, your sister, and the others are doing."

"Well, I've been on the streets myself, so I know what it's like."

He nodded. "Last thing I ever expected to happen to me."

"I think we've all felt that way at one time. Are you from around here?"

He shook his head. "My wife and I came out here from Ohio. I'm a computer programmer, and we figured Seattle was the place to be."

"And it wasn't?"

"Well, I was hired as a temp at Microsoft, but I didn't make enough to even pay the rent. My wife got pregnant, we quickly went through our savings, then we had to sell our car. Microsoft was using me less and less, we got evicted from our apartment, and here we are."

"How did you get interested in computers?"

"I'm a master carpenter. But I developed chronic bursitis in my wrists and elbows and had to give it up. I figured computers was where the world was heading…You into computers?"

"Me?" Jackson laughed. "I don't know a piece of software from a hardon."

Mark laughed. "That's funny."

At Salty's, they met up with Joe, and the three of them loaded the pickup with boxes of food: fresh fruit, pastries, packages of sausages and bacon and dozens of eggs.

Back at Tent City as they started unloading the food, a late model Ford station wagon suddenly pulled up beside the pickup. Inside were four young men. A man in the front passenger seat rolled down the window, and called out:

"Why don't you lazy assholes get a job?"

Jackson replied without thinking: "I don't need a job, I have a life."

"Ignore them," Mark warned, continuing to unload.

But it was too late for that. Already the four men were hastily stepping out of their vehicles.

Astonished, Jackson and Mark stepped back as the four men started picking out the boxes of food, emptying them into the street. One of the men opened up one of the egg cartons and started throwing eggs at Mark and Jackson, laughing gleefully.

Jackson noticed that across the street at the curb in front of "The Pathfinder Bookstore" was a Seattle police department vehicle with two of Mayor Schell's finest inside watching the proceedings, and doing nothing about it.

Jackson was incredulous. "What the fuck!" he pondered out loud, dodging another egg.

One of the men grabbed an apple and took a bite. He said: "We're an environmental organization. We're cleaning up the neighborhood of you lazy assholes that don't work!"

The others in the encampment were running over. Mark put his arms up to the Tent City people frantically, as if to hold them back. "Leave them alone!" he ordered. "Just ignore them."

Responding involuntarily to Mark's leadership, they drew back.

The man holding the apple signaled them to come hither with waves of his hands, daring the Tent City people to fight.

For a moment everyone just stood there staring at one another, a Mexican standoff.

"Why don't you people just leave!" Caitlin yelled.

The food from the pickup was spread all over the street, boxes tossed on the parking strip or into the avenue. The four men got back into their car and squirreled away.

Mark began picking up the boxes in the avenue, and the others in the encampment began following suit, cleaning up the mess. The police car slowly drove off.

"It's a good thing we didn't get into a brawl," Mark said. "The pigs are looking for any excuse to come in here and break up the camp by hauling us all to jail."

"Why'd they do that?" Caitlin said, totally at a loss to understand what motivates some people.

"I used to do a lot of protesting in the sixties," Mark said. "I'm sure the police hired those guys, perhaps they're cops themselves. It's an old tactic, as old as Jesus."

They continued cleaning up the mess.

Then this same police vehicle returned, emergency lights flashing. They got out of their vehicle and cited the encampment for littering.

THIRTY-THREE

It was the summer of 1996. Peter and Perry were at the cabin in Chelan. Perry said to Peter: "Let's go for a run."

Running alongside the familiar road that undulated north on the east side of the 55-mile fjord that was erroneously called a lake, Perry said: "I have something to tell you."

"All right."

"I'm sick."

"How sick? You don't look sick."

"I am. I'm very sick. I have hepatitis C."

"Hepatitis C? I've never heard of hepatitis C. I've heard of A and B, but not C."

"I had never heard of it either. I don't know if you remember, but I got it when I was using heroin."

"That must have been more than twenty-five years ago. That was hepatitis C?"

He nodded. "When I went to see the doctor about it back then because I was badly jaundiced, he said it was a strain of hepatitis they were seeing a lot in kids then but it hadn't been identified. But he said since I was already jaundiced, the disease was already coming to an end, so not to worry about it. And he was right; I got better, as you know. Until now. Since then they have developed a name for it: Hepatitis C. And since then there have been other strains discovered, D, E, F, maybe more."

"How long have you known this?"

"About a year ago I began having joint pains. I was feeling weak and tired. My workouts weren't going well. I'd drink a couple beers and become nauseated. I went to my doctor, and he took blood tests. He said I had alarmingly elevated liver enzymes and sent me to a liver specialist. The liver specialist took more blood tests, and said I had Hepatitis C. He did an ultrasound and a liver biopsy. He said I was in trouble, that if I didn't get a liver transplant, I would be dead within five years."

"What!"

"So I went to another specialist for a second opinion. He gave a completely different diagnosis. He said they were seeing a lot of hepatitis C in patients these days, but most people lived out pretty normal lives despite it, and that I would probably die from something else before the virus got me, so not to worry about it."

"Sounds to me like they all got their heads up their arses."

"They're in a learning curve in regard to this virus. Anyway, I went for a third opinion, and the third liver specialist confirmed the diagnosis of the first specialist, saying I needed a liver transplant as soon as possible."

"This after nearly thirty years?"

"Apparently the gestation period can last that long."

"So what now?"

"I'm on the list for a transplant. But it's a complicated process. Those who are sickest are given priority. This makes sense, except if someone is too sick they wouldn't be able to endure the trauma of a transplant. So I have to be in just the right position to be selected, and then someone who's a donor with a liver compatible to mine has to die somewhere. It's a crap shoot."

Back at the cabin Perry continued on about the disease. It was more rampant than AIDS. Millions of people had it and didn't know they had it. It was contacted through an exchange of blood, like AIDS. The most common means of transplant was through an infected needle. Those who had tattoos from tattoo artists who didn't sterilize their needles properly transferred it. People who got transfusions got it. Those who snorted cocaine got it from sharing straws. And it could be contacted through sex. Obituaries of people who were said to have died from "liver disease" likely had Hepatitis C. Ray Charles died from it. Allen Ginsberg died from it. Because of the long gestation period, many die from something else before they get sick from it. Many have no symptoms. Many may even drink to excess and their livers are fine. They were the lucky ones. It was indiscriminate. "I'm one of the unlucky ones," Perry said. "But nevertheless, more people will die from hepatitis C than from AIDS."

THIRTY-FOUR

Going for a walk with Joeboy, Jackson came upon a garage sale. He spotted a beat-up old Diamond Back mountain bike with a $50 price tag on it.

"Mind if I test it out?" Jackson said.

"Not at all."

He rode up the street shifting gears, Joeboy running alongside playfully. He rounded the corner, and felt a temptation to just keep on riding. He would have at one time. This time he went back and gave the lady fifty dollars. She seemed surprised that he didn't try to talk her down. The bike was a piece of shit.

He rode it home, Joeboy loping alongside. He washed it, cleaned the gummed up chain with kerosene, then sprinkled it with chain oil. He pumped up the tires.

He rode his bike everywhere, to the grocery store, to the bank, to the post office, to the video store. Everywhere he went in the neighborhood, he rode his bike, Joeboy running beside him at heel. He rode through Lincoln Park, Fauntleroy Park, Schmitz Park, Westcrest, and Camp Long, taking in the symmetry of the landscape and pushing himself hard, feeling the resistance against his buttocks, thighs, hamstrings, and calves.

When he got home he did pushups and sit-ups, then yoga stretches. He did this almost every day, and in a couple months he was able to do 200 sit-ups and 50 pushups without stopping.

His pants became baggy as he shed weight and felt his long-abused body grow tight with muscle.

After he exercised, he sat on a cushion and meditated for twenty minutes, concentrating on his breathing and the expansion of his diaphragm.

Afterwards he rewarded himself with a cup of coffee, a joint, and a cigarette.

Winter passed into spring, and when the sun finally dried out the northwest terrain appropriately enough, he bicycled to Big 5 and bought a Prince Graphite Wide Body tennis racket on sale for $59.95 regularly $189.95 and a couple cans of Penn tennis balls, strapped them on his bike rack, and biked down to the Lincoln Park tennis courts and banged the ball against the bang board, Joeboy trying to run down the ball.

He concentrated on his forehand, backhand, then serve. He did this for half an hour, then stretched, and then sat on the bench watching the others play, many of whom he recognized when he played here years ago with Peter and Hoge. Amazingly, they looked the same, as if the years of exercise on the courts stunted the aging process.

Peter was a natural athlete and a good tennis player, but Jackson had sometimes held his own against him even with his alcohol-diseased body.

He continued this routine for two or three weeks on the days it wasn't raining, riding his bike down to the courts, Joeboy jogging alongside. He concentrated on a spot on the wall like a Buddhist with his archery set, hitting the ball with a mantra-like grunt. He concentrated on his form, bringing the racket back, bending his knees, connecting the ball with a racket, following through as he straightened his legs.

When he thought it was time, he telephoned Peter and asked him out to hit.

They met at the courts, and Peter looked at him in shock.

"How much weight have you lost?"

"I don't know. I haven't weighed myself."

"You look ten years younger."

Peter, on the other hand, seemed to have aged considerably. He was still fit, but his face was shadowed with a cloud of worry, his forehead crosshatched with wrinkles, his black eyes supporting pockets of weariness. He carried an anguished look.

They played a match and Jackson won, 7-5, 6-4. Peter was stunned. "What's happened to you?"

"Sobriety has happened to me."

———

One of these days while using the bang board, lost in concentration with the ball and racket, someone approached.

"Would you like to hit?"

He was startled away from his concentration, and the ball ricocheted off the frame and sailed over the fence to the south courts.

"I'm sorry," she said, laughing. "I didn't mean to scare you."

She was about forty, tall, taller than he; with medium cut auburn hair that danced with the slight wind, and a stylish, nicely fitting tennis outfit. She was tanned and doe-eyed, little sun wrinkles etching around her bright blue eyes. She again asked to hit.

"Sure."

She introduced herself as "Bette."

"Jackson," he said, taking her right hand.

"What's your first name?"

"That is my first name."

"Oh."

"People usually call me 'Jacky'."

They hit for about ten minutes. He was surprised at how crisp her volleys were, her sweet spot the size of a basketball.

"Wanna play a set?" Bette said.

They played a set. Jackson lost concentration watching Bette's shapely figure dancing the court. She had trouble handling his serve, but she was consistent otherwise, and had few unforced errors. Still, Jackson won, 6-4.

She seemed upset. They sat on the bench, taking a break. Jackson lit a cigarette.

"You *smoke?*" she said, incredulously.

Jackson held the toxic white stick out in front of himself despairingly. "Can't seem to give the buggers up."

"I used to, but after I took up tennis it didn't seem to make sense."

"Tennis or no tennis—it makes no sense."

"Now I'm addicted to tennis. I play here every day it doesn't rain, and I've seen you here hitting the bang board. You looked like you could use a partner."

They played another set, and she was more determined this time. But Jackson won again, 7-5. Bette was not happy.

THIRTY-FIVE

Weather permitting, he met Bette at the courts nearly every day, finding himself blending in with a regular group that met there. As his fitness increased, his tobacco use decreased, and by July he was not smoking cigarettes at all, with no discernible withdrawal symptoms.

But he still required his two cups of coffee in the morning and a joint in the evening.

Jackson usually won his singles contests. Whether it was against the older, craftier players, or the younger more athletic ones, he found himself winning, despite the fact that he didn't particularly care if he won or not. He was so generous with his calls that even his opponents sometimes questioned whether the shots were really good.

Yet he still won. His concentration on the ball became so keen he sometimes forgot who his opponents were and what the score was, so keen that he could spot the fuzz on the ball as it spun towards him.

He almost always beat Peter now.

Tennis became Jackson's pursuit in aestheticism and meditation. He became so confident in his game that he hit away as hard as he could, the ball nearly always dropping into his opponent's court for a winner. He felt like an intelligent animal with grace, rhythm, and unnatural speed. His body responded positively to the psychology and physiology of training. Tennis became his antidote, his redemption to the abuse he had rendered his body the previous thirty years.

In doubles, nearly everyone was eager to be his partner. And the one who usually ended up being his partner was Bette. And that is when he lost his concentration, as he stood behind the service block facing her as she bent over at the net in her little white tennis outfit prepared to volley.

And he sensed a mutual attraction.

Sometimes when the matches extended into the late afternoon, Bette's boyfriend Jim arrived after he had gotten off work, and the sexual aura that hovered on the court between Jackson and Bette was broken like static on the radio, and there was a sudden awkwardness that affected each of their game. Everyone in their little tennis group was conscious of this, except Jim.

Jim was about fifty, a lean and handsome six-footer with thick silver hair. He seemed to play the game because Bette did. He tried hard, but he didn't play at the level commensurate with his efforts, certainly not well enough to satisfy Bette, who seemed irritated with his constant unforced errors when he was her partner.

When Jim didn't show, which was often, since Jim had a job—Jackson and Bette after tennis went to the Cat's Eye across the street for iced lattes and sometimes had lunch together.

Bette was a divorcee with an 18-year-old son away at college at Western State, and a 16-year-old daughter attending Kennedy High School, a parochial school in Burien. She had been married for 15 years, and from her divorce settlement inherited the home in Shorewood, with its sweeping view of Puget Sound. She didn't seem to require employment.

One day in late July, Jackson was putting his tennis gear together to bike down to the courts, and he got a phone call from Bette, asking if he could pick her up for tennis because her car was in the shop.

He parked the pickup in front of her house and followed the brick path to her front door. The door was wide open, so he wandered inside.

He saw her turned away from him bending over her tennis gear. She was wearing her little white outfit that drove him crazy. Staring at her muscular hips, exposing thin white panties, Jackson felt a stir in his loins.

Other than that one blowjob from the crack whore, he hadn't been with a woman since Jane. He reminded himself that he'd taken a vow of chastity in his quest for spiritual enlightenment. But the truth was—he just hadn't been laid in awhile. She straightened and turned, matching his stare with hers. She dropped her gear as he approached. Their scant clothing peeled away like extraneous skin. They were oblivious to the wide open front door as they grappled each other, moaning, kissing, and exploring each other's firm bodies. She pushed him to the bare hardwood floor. On top of him, her body at an angle to his prone one, he came suddenly, regrettably, but she held him tight inside of her brutally, refusing to let go as they rolled across the creaking oak, she pushing and pulling against him anxiously, her full breasts quivering, pumping him desperately until she arrived at her own climax, then pushed away from him carefully. But he put her back on the floor on all fours, her tennis-honed buttocks high in the air, forearms down, her face sideways to the floor, grimacing as if in pain. Jackson mounted, straddling each side of her hips like a wild animal, digging his fingernails into her heaving hips and leaving claw marks on each buttock, collapsing in a heap beside her.

While they lay on the floor catching their breath, the mailman came up the stairs and put mail in her mailbox. He didn't seem to notice them.

Laughing, she said: "Well, I guess we've had our warm up. Ready to play?"

THIRTY-SIX

One rainy day a month later, Bette was over at his house for the first time. After they made love she looked around at what he had inside his home, an old sofa and easy chair purchased from the Salvation Army, a beat up old dresser from a garage sale, his single bed, an end table next to it nailed and glued together from scraps of wood found in his garage, an unfinished book case purchased from B&D Unfinished Furniture on 35th and Avalon stocked with a few books bought from Pegasus Used Books in the West Seattle junction, mostly books on Buddhism. After this thoughtful stroll as he was preparing coffee, and said: "Jacky—what do you *do?*"

"I boil the water first."

She laughed. "Seriously." She sat down carefully in the wobbly old oak chair he had in the kitchen, which felt about ready to collapse under her. "What do you *do?*"

"I do the same as you do. I play tennis."

"You know what I mean: As in making a living."

After the water came to a boil, he let it settle a moment before pouring it slowly over the freshly ground beans in the carafe. His coffee preparation had become a science.

"I could ask you the same question."

"Well, actually, unfortunately, that is an issue."

"An issue?"

"I need to get a job. My savings is exhausted, and the child support I receive isn't enough to pay the bills."

"I see."

"I'm three months behind on my mortgage payment."

He slowly poured more water over the rim of the risen coffee until it condensed at the bottom of the filter. When this drained, he poured out two cups. There was a sweet, foamy brown settlement on top. He handed it to Bette.

"You're an old hippie," she declared, like an accusation.

He sipped carefully and nodded. "I've been called worse."

"This coffee is delicious!" She took another sip, savoring the rich taste. "Mmm…But you are, you're an old hippie. I've never seen you drive a car. You're always either riding your bike or driving that beat up old pickup."

"Don't say that about my pickup while you're in it."

She laughed. "Your hair is scraggly. You don't have a regular job."

"I don't have any job." He laughed.

"Have you ever?"

"Worked? Of course."

"Why don't you need to now?"

"You don't have to worry about your mortgage."

"What?"

"For now at least. I will get you caught up on your mortgage."

"You will do that? I was about to go to Jim for a loan."

"Yes, I will do that. But you can't ask any more questions."

"Why not?"

"Because I choose not to talk about why I don't work."

"I'll pay you back when I find some work."

He shrugged. "You don't have to."

"You'll do that; just give me three months worth of house payments? It'll be over three thousand."

"You're in trouble. I'll get you out of trouble."

THIRTY-SEVEN

Peter wasn't transferring into the computer age with ease, grace or dignity. He arrived at school one day to find that someone had set up some monstrosity on his desk, a cumbersome white box that looked like a TV connected with thick wires to a white monolith beneath his desk, which he had to nudge aside to make room for his long legs. He had no idea what he was supposed to do with this machinery. He didn't know how to turn it on, and what he was supposed to do with it once it was running.

And then Blanche, his literary agent, told him she could no longer accept his type- written manuscripts with their sloppy corrections and messy white-outs. Everyone was using "word" now, whatever that was.

Ever so reluctantly, he went out and purchased a computer for his home office as well. He explained to the salesperson that he was computer ignorant, and the salesperson replied, "No worries. This unit is plug and go!"

But when he took the items out of the box at home in his office and spread them out on the floor, he hadn't a clue what to do with all the wires and other apparatus. He began to read the directions, but they may as well have been written in Greek.

He panicked. His brain rammed into a brick wall. He was about to stuff it all back into the box, take it out in the back yard, and take a sledgehammer to it.

But he checked this impulse and instead called Paul, who had been using a computer at his work for a year or more. Paul came over and plugged it in easy as pie. Then he downloaded Microsoft Word and taught him how to use it.

Peter had one advantage over Paul in this regard: He knew how to type.

Still, he struggled with this new technology for a month before he was able to get back to his writing. He couldn't see how this new computer age was conducive to the creative process; to him it was only a distraction. Didn't Dostoyevsky write monumental works of fiction with just a quill pen and an inkwell? To Peter, writing was low tech. He just wanted to write; he didn't have time for all this extraneous technological bullshit that had nothing to do with the inward task of creativity.

Downtime was essential for creativity. Disruptions to his right brain thinking were a hindrance. His ADD didn't help. Peter would find the computer age a constant barrier to his creative impulses the rest of his life, as he was forced to repeatedly adapt to changing technology with increasing frequency. He would get a cell phone only when Caitlin handed it to him and subsequently cancelled their home line. He would never use text messaging. He would never use a digital camera. He would only use the cell phone, and even struggled to get used to that technology and all it entailed. He would never get a Blackberry or a Smart phone. He got a blog only when his agent told him he needed it to promote his books. He would never get an I-Pad. He would use his turntable for music the rest of his relatively short life.

What he would do with this computer, however, is finally finish his novel and have it published to high if not popular acclaim. And he wouldn't imagine having completed it without benefit of Word.

THIRTY-EIGHT

Sitting on the floor one morning in late autumn stretching after a long bike ride, Jackson for the first time managed to touch his head to his thighs without bending his knees. He was thinking of Bette. He was always thinking of Bette. She was still with her boyfriend, but she was also still with him. He had asked her to make a choice, and she had said she couldn't; she loved them both. There was so much of her that was unreachable, minuscule parts of her that he couldn't define. He couldn't seem to find the courage to break from her altogether. He had never been in love like this before. When he was drinking, the only love he had, the only desperation he felt, was for alcohol. Now it was the same with a woman, staying with someone who was no good for him. When she left his house he could smell remnants of her left behind, little reminders that shook him to the core. Unable to attach himself to her permanently, he anguished in the little lots of time allotted to him. He would remain unhappy until he could cut her off completely. Everything about her, her body, her breath, her hair, her movements on the tennis court, drove him insane. And the others at the courts knew it. He was horrified with that which gave him pleasure.

Joeboy's ears were alerted instinctively, and he jumped to his feet and barked angrily with the knock at the door, jumping up to sniff at the crack of light at the bottom of the front door. Opening the door, he was presented with a ghost.

"Hoge!"

"Hello, Jacky."

"You're alive!"

"Yes, Jacky I'm alive. Surprised?"

Jackson pulled the door wide to allow him to enter. Hoge stepped inside, a waft of stale alcohol following him. His six-foot frame stood erect in the middle of the living room looking at his surroundings as if he were house hunting. His hair was graying more but still thick. His face was bloated and his nose had grown bulbous, riddled with broken capillaries. His stomach was distended from a swollen liver. He was unshaven and scraggly, his clothes rags. Even when drunk all the time, Hoge had always before managed to be a sharp dresser. He now looked like he'd been living on the streets.

He ignored Joeboy, who was looking up at him pleadingly, tail wagging, begging for attention.

"I hear you're doin' all right for yourself these days."

"I'm well, Hoge."

"That's not what I meant." He quickly scanned the surroundings again. "I had expected more than this."

"Sit down, Hoge. I guess we need to talk."

"Got anything to drink?"

"Juice, skim milk, water."

"Got anything to drink?" he repeated.

"There is no alcohol in the house, Hoge."

Hoge nodded, taking a seat on the sofa. "Yeah, I heard ya quit drinking. I'll have some ice water."

Jackson got the ice water.

Hoge sat on the sofa by the wood burning stove, shaking as if chilled.

By the end of the afternoon, business between the two had been concluded. Jackson had transferred all his monetary interests over to Hoge. Hoge offered to let him keep a few thousand, but Jackson declined; he didn't want or need it.

FORTY-TWO

Jackson wandered into a familiar old watering hole on Capitol Hill. The name of the place didn't come to mind, but where he took a seat at the bar felt as familiar as a favorite old easy chair. The place looked the same. The smell and the warmth was the same. The people he didn't recognize, but nevertheless were the same.

He ordered bourbon, neat. The drink was set before him, but he didn't drink it. He realized with a nostalgic sadness that he didn't really want it, that whatever scant pleasure he had once derived from the indulgence of alcohol was past, and could never be recaptured.

Bette was getting married to Jim. He thought maybe one drunk could assuage the pain somewhat. But he knew differently now. He continued to stare into his drink.

"Hello, McMahon."

Jackson looked up at a very large man whom at first he did not recognize.

"Forget who I am little buddy."

"McCann!" He smiled at him, once recognizing him, as one welcomes an old friend.

"That's right, McMahon. It's McCann."

"I've been looking all over town for you, man!"

"I'm a tolerant dude, McMahon. You fuck me over once, I'm willing to forgive. But I *never* forget. Fuck me over twice…"

Jackson's mind instinctively raced. He knew he could talk his way out of this, like he'd done a thousand times before. McCann was easy. But instead, he said:

"Wow. Karma."

———

Jackson's eyelids slowly pried open. A blur gradually focused. Something pushed on his body like an unbearable weight. He struggled to move, couldn't. He arched his back and tried to spread his legs. He couldn't. He pondered who he was.

"Jacky," said Caitlin. Behind her, stood Peter.

His eyes traversed a blurry white room. It was unfamiliar, as unfamiliar as his numb body.

"You're in Harborview, Jacky."

"I…I…" He tried to think, but nothing came to mind. Movement brought sudden pain, excruciating pain.

"Don't talk, Jacky. You're going to be all right. The guy who did this to you is sitting in jail waiting for you to press charges. He was beating you to death. It took four men to get him off you."

"I…I don't want to press charges."

"We'll talk about that later."

"I deserved it."

"We'll worry about all that later, when you're better…You've been hurt pretty bad."

"Caitlin…" He tried to sit up, and was again stricken with agonizing pain. "*Aaah*"

"Just rest, Jacky. Don't try to move."

"I didn't drink, Caiti."

Caitlin smiled, and rested her hand softly on his belly. "That's good, Jacky."

"Hoge."

"Hoge? What about Hoge?"

"Hoge…"

"I know the whole story, Jacky. He's been all over West Seattle telling everyone you took his Lotto money."

Jackson closed his eyes. He felt extremely tired. He exposed his left arm, and Caitlin grabbed his hand and clutched it to her bosom.

"When you're outa here," she said, "you're moving in with us until you completely recover."

Jackson rolled his eyes from side to side. "Burden."

She squeezed his hand tight. "You won't be a burden, just the opposite. I intend to keep you busy around the place."

Jackson looked up at her. She was smiling down on him. She seemed miles away. "Joeboy," he said.

"Joeboy's at our house. Hoge dropped him off."

"Hoge did that?"

"Yes."

"He's a good man, Caiti."

"He's a drunk."

"He has a disease."

"Yes, and he'll go through all that Lotto money and drink himself to death."

"Maybe not."

Suddenly Jackson was seized with a sharp, gasping pain. He couldn't breathe.

"What is it? Are you all right?"

"*Pain!*" he gasped.

It radiated to his extremities. Nausea rose from his stomach; a projectile of blood spewed all over the white sheet before him.

"*Jesus!*" Peter said, and ran out of the room to get someone, while Caitlin pushed frantically at the nurse's alert button.

His torso rose involuntarily from the bed; he was hyperventilating. His mind whirred in confusion, lost within another plane of existence, reverting, recalling.

Caitlin rushed to the door. "*Nurse! Doctor! Someone! For God's sake!*"

"*God!*" Jackson whispered, gasping for air. "*God forgive me!*"

Caitlin rushed back to her brother, observed in horror as he slipped into convulsions. She was screaming. "*Why is no one coming!*" She pushed his shoulders down, desperately trying to calm the terrifying spasms.

Then he was still.

Finally, a nurse came running in, Peter trailing her as Caitlin clutched frantically at his immobile body.

Jackson hovered above it all, receding from the room as if sucked into a tunnel. He was calm, enlightened, at peace, his being in transformation.

FORTY-THREE

There was a woman Peter saw on occasion beginning in high school until they were both the age of fifty. He had dated her briefly in high school, then again after returning from Vietnam close to the time he met Caitlin. Then after he married Caitlin he would see her on occasion when she was married to her first husband, and then later when she was married to her second husband.

This woman's name was Christine. She is the same woman mentioned at the beginning of this history who had a remarkable likeness to the actress Charlotte Rampling.

At the twenty-year high school reunion, Christine shuffled up to him when he was alone a moment and showed him a photograph of a handsome young man. "He's your son," she said.

"What!"

"It happened while I was with Michael." Michael was her first husband.

"Why didn't you tell me!"

"I needed my husband to think the child was his, of course."

He studied the photo. He was stunned to realize that he indeed looked a lot like a Placik. "Are you sure?"

"My husband was only my height. My son is six-four."

Since Christine was five-foot-nine and Peter was six-foot-two, this made sense.

"I can't believe you've never told me before."

"I never felt the need to."

"Then why now?"

She gestured at their surroundings. "I don't know. It seemed like the appropriate time."

Peter shook his head. He never ceased to be amazed at all the ironies and twisted coincidences of life. "My God, Christine."

Before the era of cell phones, for years Christine and Peter carried pagers for the sole purpose of paging each other when one or the other could get away. These assignations would take place wherever was convenient, usually at a particular motel by the airport which supplied access to porno.

Their relationship was based almost exclusively on sex. There was a scant element of sentimentality in their affair, but for the most part they got together to fuck each other's brains out. Neither of them felt any particularly strong romantic inclination for the other, since sometimes months would go by without seeing each other, nor would they miss each other, other than for the sex. They each felt the sex was the best sex each had ever had. One summer day looking for a particular private spot in which to have sex in Camp Long, a park in West Seattle, he was so vertiginous with lust for her that he had to sit a moment. Literally, he was so dizzy with desire that he nearly fainted. Christine found this hilarious. That was the extent of her mastery over him; but beyond that, frankly, she bored him. She was pedestrian, politically apathetic and ignorant, read romance novels, and watched soap operas. After the sex was concluded, she irritated him, and he felt the desperate need to get away. Christine likely felt the same.

They talked frequently of having a threesome, mostly as a fantasy, since they were never to discover this third party benefactor. There was one friend of hers in whom trust was complete, and the friend agreed to participate, but for some reason it never came to fruition.

But unlike the famous actress, Christine didn't age well, and by age fifty, she became unattractive to him. Looking at her now it had become impossible for him to remember the lineaments of her previous beauty. He felt like he was dating an elderly woman. While like Peter, she did work out and managed to maintain a firm body free of the cellulite of which many other women seemed afflicted, her face had suddenly become old and unattractive. He wondered if she felt the same about him, because when he quit responding to her cell phone calls, the calls to him suddenly stopped as well. He was rather surprised that she gave up so easily. Perhaps she'd had another lover by then, since sex was as essential to Christine as the air, and he knew she didn't have it with her husband. As far as his son, he had never known him, and had no desire to ever know him.

And in fact, as Peter aged, his womanizing diminished, as did the admiring glances from pretty young women, along with his graying and receding hairline. He was stunned to realize one day that his students had quit flirting with him.

And then, all of a sudden, his womanizing had come to an end. For some inexplicable reason, he had lost the desire for anyone but Caitlin, and the love of his family. He felt a vague nostalgia for this sudden loss of extracurricular sex.

About this same time Peter developed an irritation in his lower right abdomen, a bloated nauseated feeling. It didn't go away, so he consulted his doctor. His doctor ordered blood tests, and could find nothing unusual other than slightly elevated LDL cholesterol, and recommended statins.

He next consulted a gastroenterologist who ordered an ultra sound, performed a colonoscopy, and an endoscopy. There was a polyp discovered in his large intestine, but nothing was discovered that could be causing the discomfort.

"Then what is it?"

The doctor shrugged and said, "Sometimes as we get older we get these aches and pains that are difficult to pinpoint."

We, Kimo Sabe? Peter thought, since the gastroenterologist was about thirty.

He then consulted a Naturopath, who after looking at his blood work, said:

"You have elevated liver enzymes," she declared matter of factly.

"What! Why didn't my doctor say anything?"

"Probably because it's only on the high end of normal. But it's higher than what I would like to see. And you have elevated bilyrubin levels."

"Bilyrubin? What's that?"

"It's bile processed by the liver. Yours is a little high, 2.0. Not bad but slightly more than normal. Do you drink much?"

This alarmed Peter enough to quit drinking—for awhile.

The pain in his abdomen ceased.

FORTY-FOUR

Perry, on the other hand, continued to deteriorate. He could no longer go running, but he forced himself to go for walks every day. Peter accompanied him, and also to roundtable discussions with those who had received liver transplants and those who were waiting to receive them. The ones who received transplants all said that their lives had improved considerably almost immediately after receiving the transplant. It was a like a pep talk for those who were waiting.

It had become too late for Perry to receive the interferon treatment currently being administered to hep C patients. The side effects of the treatment were so severe that his body could not have tolerated them. The doctors as usual had latently recognized the seriousness of Perry's condition.

Peter urged Perry to try medicinal herbs such as milk thistle, dandelion, and turmeric that esteemed health practitioners such as Andrew Weil said could actually heal a cirrhotic liver. Perry still refused, on the advice of his doctors—doctors who as far as Peter could tell, were doing nothing to make Perry better.

He became rail thin, except in his abdomen, which was distended from his enlarged liver. He became jaundiced. His compromised immune system resulted in maladies such as fungal infections in his toenails and fingernails. He became confused, disoriented. He said, "What?" when no one had said anything.

One day at his house walking Perry out to Peter's car, Perry staggered like his legs were made of rubber. He collapsed on the sidewalk and bloodied his nose. Peter helped him up and back into the house. Peter gave him a towel for his nose. When the bleeding had stopped, he put on latex gloves and put the bloody towel in the wash with bleach. He went to the bathroom and scrubbed his hands with soap and scalding water, paranoid of contacting the infected blood. He looked at himself in the mirror and broke into a flood of tears over the callousness of his self-worry, and pity for his brother. He dried the tears, not about to let Perry see his purge of emotion. The Placik's were not allowed to express or experience familial emotion. They kept it bottled up, reticent, inexpressive, stoic. They were not an affectionate family. When their father died, they stoically went through the motions of grief. No one wept, not even their mother.

Then, miraculously it seemed, a donor with a compatible liver died in an auto accident in Fairbanks, Alaska. The liver was flown to Seattle and at midnight Perry was at the University of Washington Hospital undergoing a transplant. Everyone was euphoric. He would get better. He would have twenty, perhaps even thirty more years of productive life. They would be back on the tennis court this summer.

But something was wrong. Instead of getting better he got sicker. A month later the family was summoned into a hospital conference room and informed that the virus had attacked the transplanted liver and Perry had a blood infection.

"I don't understand," Peter said. "Why did you do the transplant?"

The doctor shook his head, looking dismayed. "There was something wrong with the transplanted liver…It was compromised somehow…infected… I don't know…"

"If you don't know, who does?"

Perry lay semi-conscious; his once six-foot-two inches shrunk into a gaunt bag of bones, looking like an elderly man, his suddenly graying hair sparse wisps, his jaundiced body gasping for air. When they talked to him, he responded with weak gestures and grunts. He was only 53. It was not right.

He seemed like someone else. The yellow skeletal body gasped for air. His face was contorted in a grimace of pain. The sound of his gasping filled the room with horror.

Peter asked a nurse if he was on morphine.

"He's not in pain!" she replied cheerfully.

218

"You have no idea the pain he's in."

The nurse's smiley-face faded.

"I want him on morphine."

The nurses and orderlies bustled about uselessly. *What is the point of all this?* Peter pondered. *We die, and they do nothing about it.* The liver specialists no longer bothered to show their humiliated faces. The experiment was over. It was on to other patients for more useless experiments.

The ugliness, horror, and injustice of it infuriated Peter. The minutes stretched into hours. Peter paced the hallway, wanting to hurt someone, wanting to hurl a doctor through a window, wanting someone to pay for this injustice. He felt his blood pressure rising as he seethed. Why Perry of all people? Why not him instead? If he could trade in his useless life to save Perry, he would do so in an instant.

As the gray day surrendered to darkness, the family gathered around his bed and waited for the end.

Perry's wife brought a priest. Perry protested, squirming and gesticulating frantically, until she took the poor Father away. Perry wouldn't give up, that was the thing. Until his dying breath, he never gave up.

Perry was a follower. He was intelligent, witty, and funny—and he was a follower. He was popular and handsome, the most handsome of the three handsome Placik brothers. Everyone loved him. But he was a follower. He had followed his high school mates into heroin use.

Then he had followed Peter into tennis, bicycling, and running—and proceeded to surpass Peter in all three of these athletic endeavors. He was an aggressive athlete. He pushed himself to the limit in foot races, running sub-six-minute miles in 10K's, seven-minute-miles in marathons. At tennis, he usually hit top-spin, seldom underspin—forehand and backhand. He had a Sampras-like overhead slam, his body soaring into the air like Michael Jordon to smash the ball. He was always looking to go to the net. Win or lose, he was always going for it. He never played a defensive game, on or off the court. To his dying breath, he was always looking to come to the net.

At last, they watched the final death gasp. The horrid death rattle had ceased. The weeping stopped and they stood silently and reverently. In death Perry finally rested, relieved of his suffering. It was quiet and calm.

Peter felt like Perry had been a guinea pig. He thought about the interferon treatment he could have received early on. He thought about the medicinal herbs he could have ingested. He thought about the transplanted liver that had only facilitated his death. Unlike with Jackson, Peter didn't go through the proper stages of grief. He stayed angry the rest of his life, which was seven more years.

FORTY-FIVE

At the age of 62 Peter retired to collect his pension and Social Security. He should have been happy about this. But instead, suddenly and inexplicably, he was seized by a deep depression—or something—something so horrible he was unable to describe it or express it on page. What he used to refer to as one of his "moods" was now an internal storm that tore at his soul and physical being.

Naturally, he had been depressed by the deaths of his best friend and of his brother. He was depressed by his failing body on the tennis court, of the refusal of his aching limbs to respond properly to the simple bouncing ball. He was depressed by the failure of his writing to receive the recognition he craved, if not deserved. *Oldone* had received rave reviews, but few people had bought it, and he hadn't recovered even his publisher's advance. But it was more than that, he couldn't pinpoint it exactly.

For one thing, he could no longer drink. He had always depended on alcohol as a stress relief. He was not like Jackson, who once told Peter that he didn't enjoy drinking. Peter had enjoyed it, every minute of it, even the queasy feeling in the morning that seemed to ironically give him a lively boost of energy. He enjoyed the way it made him feel and act. Alcohol was a soothing agent, better than any meds he had ever been prescribed. He realized his depression had coincided with his withdrawal from alcohol.

Suddenly, at the age of 62, this medicinal agent, this recreational inebriant, no longer eased his emotional pains. Instead, even one drink induced nausea, a strange visceral uneasiness. He assumed his body was telling him: Enough.

Caitlin was happy that he had quit drinking. But his emotions seemed not up to the task. Furthermore, a strange anxiety afflicted him during the night when he was trying to sleep. He was baffled by an almost psychedelic altering of consciousness, as if the indulgence of the sixties was resurfacing from the recesses of several decades ago.

Alcohol was supposed to be a depressant. Why then was he depressed without it? Whether sunny or gray outside, he was perpetually gray inside, and this grayness was exacerbated by physical pain, in his joints and in his gut.

He struggled through his runs, but they became too much, and he had to stop. His once muscular frame shrank, except around his belly, where he developed a disgusting layer of fat.

———

One day he and Caitlin went for their usual walk on Alki. He looked out among the calm blue bay and across to the city shrouded with a white mist, and decided he was feeling better. He had always loved Alki, and had never wanted to live anywhere else. He loved all the seasons here. In the autumn, the city was saturated in yellows and reds, the deciduous trees stripped of wet, decaying leaves by the brisk wind, except in the Seattle parks, which were dense with Evergreens. In the winter the misty, moderate rains kept the land a deep green. In the spring there was a fresh breeze that coincided with new life, the new shoots, the blossoms and the singing birds. The summers were neither too hot nor too cold, but nearly perfect.

But the next day the depression returned with even more unbearable anguish.

———

Then one day he felt a lump on the left side of his neck. It was about an inch in circumference and protruded about a quarter of an inch. He went to his family physician, and she told him what he had already suspected, that it was a swollen lymph node. She said it was probably a virus or an infection, and that it would probably go away in a couple of weeks.

When it didn't, his doctor sent him to an otalaryngolist, who told him while sticking a needle in the swollen lymph node for a biopsy that, "There is a significant possibility this is cancer."

"No shit," Peter said. "That's scary."

"Yes."

And a few days later Doctor Rowland called and confirmed that the biopsy was positive.

"What kind?"

"We don't know until we do more tests. We'll have to look for the primary source. But since it's in your lymph nodes it's already in stage four."

"Jesus."

Doctor Rowland was very matter of fact, a part of his personality that Peter would come to appreciate. He had never been fond of condescending medical practitioners. He had been disgusted with the medical team treating Perry like a child when he had been dying.

"It's probably somewhere in the base of your tongue or in your throat. We've been seeing a lot of people coming in with a particular kind of cancer called squamous cell carcinoma that is caused by the Human Papillomavirus virus. The virus is from sex that infects the genital area, but also the throat and mouth from oral sex. Most adults who have this virus don't know it since there oftentimes are no symptoms. But it causes cervical cancer in women and now they are thinking that it is causing oral cancer in men, in the squamous cells in the mouth, tongue, and throat. It can also cause anal cancer from being infected from anal sex. If it isn't treated it will metastasize to the esophagus and lungs. There also is a small possibility it is thyroid cancer, but as I say, we'll have to do more tests. You will have a PET scan, and then there will be more biopsies."

"What's the treatment?"

"If it's what I think it is, it will involve 35 daily radiation sessions and three chemotherapy treatments. This type of chemo doesn't make the hair fall out, and there are drugs for nausea, but that and the radiation will make you very weak and tired. The radiation will cause a very bad burn on your neck and your throat will be very sore. You will have to receive pain meds, and your throat may become so constricted that it might require a feeding tube placed in your stomach…But let's not jump the gun; we'll wait for the results of the PET scan.

"Are there any questions?"

Peter was too stunned to think of any at the moment. The doctor told Peter to compile a list of questions for when Peter and his wife met with others on the team to discuss the treatment schedule.

A week later he had a PET scan. The next day Doctor Rowland called and said that hot spots had been detected in the base of his tongue and in his esophagus. They would schedule him for surgery.

The following day he met with the radiation oncologist, and they ran the same scenario by him that Doctor Rowland did. When they said it would likely result in a feeding tube in his stomach, he said:

"I can't do that."

"I'm afraid you may have no choice."

"Sure I do."

"And what is that, Peter?" Caitlin said.

"To lie down and go to sleep."

"I know it sounds formidable," Doctor Herstein said. "And it is. But we have drugs to maintain the pain, even morphine if necessary. It won't be as bad as it seems."

Peter couldn't imagine any kind of pain medication that would allow him to tolerate that severe of a treatment, which would likely last for months, he was told, since it would continue long after the radiation treatments had ceased.

A week later Doctor Rowland performed surgery to look for the "primary source." When he came out of surgery, he was told him that tumors had been discovered in his left tonsil and esophagus which were likely the primary source, but it wouldn't be confirmed until they did biopsies.

Two days later Doctor Rowland called and said it was confirmed, he had cancers in his tonsil and esophagus. They would schedule him for treatment.

Throughout Peter's life he was for the most part considered mild-mannered, placid, and shy. But when he was in one of his "moods", he could fall into an inexplicable rage. His brothers and his father were the same. Growing up in West Seattle, the Placik Brothers had a "reputation". There were no Pollack jokes around any of the Placik's, not if anyone wanted to maintain their health.

And when he was in one of these states of depression, he walked around with a dark cloud imbedded into his features.

The next night, unable to sleep at two a.m. and overwhelmed with this incorrigible rage, he got up and fixed himself a stiff shot of Canadian whiskey. He took a small sip, smacked his lips, relishing the sweet taste. He downed it all at once then felt the lovely rush of stress relief to his consciousness. He paused for a moment, and began to feel sick. He rushed to pour another drink. He emptied the pain pills three or four at a time down his throat with each sweet delicious swallow. He poured more whiskey. He drank. He sat down with *The Great Gatsby*, a novel he had read twenty times or more and each time got more out of it. If there is a heaven there better be literature. He read:

"Gatsby believed in the green light, the orgiastic future that year by year recedes before us. It eluded us then, but that's no matter—tomorrow we will run faster, stretch our arms farther…And one fine morning…

"So we beat on, boats against the current, borne back ceaselessly into the past."

He closed the book and wept. He meant to leave a note for Caitlin, but suddenly felt extremely tired. He lay down on the sofa and closed his eyes.

———

At the same time that Peter had retired, Paul also was forced into retirement at the age of 51 because osteoarthritis prevented him from building his furniture anymore. When once he could pound a sixteen penny nail with two swings of the hammer with his powerful right arm, now it was excruciating to swing even a finishing hammer. His hands at one time were so powerful he could crack a walnut between his huge thumb and forefinger. No more. This was no problem financially, since the family was set in that regard. But it depressed him that he was no longer able to do that which he loved. He assuaged his pain and depression with food, tramadol, injections of Embril, and a nightly six pack of Redhook beer. His body weight shot up to 300 pounds; his cholesterol was about the same. One morning Paul's wife Rosalie came home from the market and found her husband's face buried in his fried eggs and sausage, his body as still and cold as a piece of frozen winter driftwood on Alki.

FORTY-SIX

In September of 2030 a young English Lit professor sat down at the old oak desk in his new office at the University of Washington. He opened up the drawers to air out the musty smell, and in one of these drawers he saw a book. He picked it out of the drawer, and blew the dust off of it. It was called *Oldone*, by Peter Placik. Not recognizing the author, he replaced the book in the drawer and forgot about it, until a few weeks later with nothing to read he happened to see it again, and started reading. Once he began it was all he could do to put it down. The prose reminded him of Faulkner, or Wolfe. He finished the 550 pages in a weekend of marathon reading. It was the best anti-war novel he had read since *All Quiet on the Western Front*. It was also the most precise and true prose he had ever read about the Love Generation.

He researched Peter Placik on the internet and discovered that he was a writer of this novel and a book of short stories. He tried to find the book of short stories on Amazon and other sites, but found out that it was out of print and unavailable. But also while googling Peter Placik he found out where he apparently lived.

He drove to the house on Alki Avenue in West Seattle and knocked on the door. An elderly woman obviously afflicted with osteoporosis answered the door.

"Yes?"

"Mrs. Placik?"

"Yes?"

"You are Peter Placik's wife?"

"Yes?"

"I'm sorry if I'm bothering you, Mrs. Placik, but I'm wondering if I could speak with your husband."

"And you are?"

"Oh, I'm sorry, how rude of me. I'm Richard Anderson, and I believe your husband used to be a professor in the same office I'm occupying now at the University of Washington."

"I see."

"It's brilliant."

"I'm sorry?" She looked confused.

"I'm sorry—his novel…It's fantastic."

"Oh yes, I suppose it is. But you see, Mister Anderson, my husband died in 2011."

"Oh! I am sorry."

"You needn't be apologizing all the time, Mister Anderson. Is there anything else?"

"You wouldn't happen to have his book of short stories, would you?"

She paused a moment, and then opened the door wide. "Come in."

He sat down on the sofa, and Caitlin slowly shuffled out of the room. She was well under five feet in height.

Ten or fifteen minutes passed, and Richard Anderson wondered if she had forgotten him. But then she returned and handed him a book with arthritic, trembling hands.

He looked it over for a few seconds, then turned it over to read the back page. The photo of Peter Placik showed an extremely handsome man. "Do you mind if I borrow it?"

"You can have it. I have several copies in my library."

"Are you sure?"

"Would you like some coffee or tea, Mister Anderson?"

"I would love either coffee or tea, Mrs. Placik."

He read the first short story while Caitlin fixed tea. He was not able to believe that a writer who could write prose this beautifully and have this much insight into human character would be allowed to go out of print.

Professor Anderson would leave Mrs. Placik's carrying three cardboard boxes full of manuscripts, many of them type written on an old manual typewriter. Some of the pages would be so yellowed and brittle with age they would practically disintegrate in his hands while reading them.

Nevertheless, he would manage to copy most of them down into his computer and send them off to his literary agent in attachments.

The following years Peter Placik would become a posthumous literary legend. Three more books of his short stories would be released, two of them making it to the top ten of the New York Times best seller list. He also would be able to compile a list of Placik's haphazard notes and various scribbles into a novel about a bipolar Don Juan, and that too would become a best seller and winner of the Pulitzer Prize. Caitlin had died by then, but her two sons and their families became rich, which was fortunate for them, since both families had been in dire straights financially and were about to declare bankruptcy. But that's another story, and not a happy one, revolving primarily around acute alcoholism.

Around this same time, a well known furniture maker in town browsed through an antique store in Pioneer Square and was stunned by the craftsmanship of a dining room set that was on sale for $500. Looking underneath the table he was unable to detect even one flaw, and saw a stencil burnt into the underside of the table that read: *Paul Placik, furniture maker.* He did not recognize the name, but he recognized a pure craftsmanship at least equal to that of a Stickley.

He talked the owner of the antique store down to $300 for a set that had originally sold for $7,000.

The End of our Saga

Made in the USA
Charleston, SC
07 December 2013